Best wishes

Philip O. Jung

The Soul in There

PHILIP O. JUNG

COMMONGOOD PUBLISHING COMPANY
Grand Rapids, Michigan

 Published in the United States of America by CommonGood Publishing Company, 2975 Lake Drive, S.E. Grand Rapids, Michigan 49506.

orders@commongood.com

ISBN: 0-9768689-1-1

Cover model: Kyle Rasch
Cover photograph and author's photo by Susan Boomgaard
Interior design by Michelle VanGeest
Cover design by Susan Harring

The repeated couplet in "The Long, Dark Evening" is from Cracker, "Wedding Day," in *Gentleman's Blues,* Virgin Records, 1998.

For Joni
Thank you

Much gratitude to my readers and critics:
Sue Boomgaard
Keith Longberg
Ed Rutowski
Dean Salisbury
Barbara Saunier
Kim Wyngarden

At present the killing of a fox except by a pack of foxhounds is regarded with horror; but you may and do kill children in a hundred and fifty ways provided you do not shoot them or set a pack of dogs on them.

—G.B. Shaw, "Parents and Children"

[I]f we can have a fleeting experience of epiphanic enchantment, it is art and art alone that allows us to communicate it to others. Indeed, in most cases art causes it to gush out of nothingness, thus giving a meaning to our existence.

—Umberto Eco, *History of Beauty*

CONTENTS

THE ENDLESS HOUR

All around Jerry Hempstead's head the spirit of fear buzzed like a maddened deerfly, and he wasn't sure that he'd ever ride out of it or even whether there'd ever be an ever to ride into again. There were a good number of things he wasn't sure of this afternoon: where his car was in this enormous parking garage, what time it was, whether Janna would wait for him to come home before eating supper, whether or not a storm was brewing out there, why he was so afraid and of what, what was causing that horrible series of prickles in his back like teasing thumbtacks, where he had just come from, who that lovely young woman was sitting on the bench in the park at the foot of the garage, just sitting there with a notebook in her lap and unwittingly eliciting in him as he rode past her a nearly trembling awe, he was unsure of all these things. He just didn't know. "Where the hell am I?" he kept saying to himself.

More disturbing, though, were the noises thudding his eardrums, sudden screeches and rumbles, the din of disembodied voices, sirens, horns, whooshes and roars, coughing sounds. Pulsing tinny whines. Metallic drips. Grumbles. It seemed to him that with every rotation of his bike pedals a new blast of dissonance would knock him off balance, even force him now and again to veer into the path of an oncoming car or into the trailer hitch behind a three-axle pickup truck sticking out of its parking spot like a malevolent leg in a grade school aisle. And each time in his swerve of avoidance he'd end up overcompensating with a sudden twist of the handlebars turning the front wheel at a ninety degree angle and having to catch himself or fall off the bike. Here he was, a balding new senior barely five years into his AARP membership, of barely medium height, forced into the ungainly posture of preventing an outright fall onto the inimical pavement of this insidious garage by tiptoeing along, struggling to maintain the bike's equilibrium, the horizontal bar between seat and front wheel barely touching his most loyal and truest, if at times capricious, little friends, his mouth agape breathlessly uttering furious warnings to himself—and repeating this charade at least once on every ascending ramp.

If only the motorists passing him were the exclusive spectators of this amusing display Jerry wouldn't have felt so foolish. But always there were the pedestrians too—women with preschoolers, businesspeople, college students—either looking for their vehicle or just slamming the doors and entering the traffic lane on foot and always, it seemed, only a few yards away from his dignity rolling like a bowling ball past their toes. For the benefit of these innocent citizens, each trying to maintain some sense of stability and privacy in the tumult of parking garage clamor, he struggled to keep the curses that spewed automatically with each loss of his balance to at most a raspy whisper, but at times a rousing "Jesus Christ alfuckingmighty!" or a "Holy fuckin' A!" would assault them in spite of his best effort. It wasn't so much the looks of disapproval or even astonishment of the adults that bothered him after such outbursts, but the horrified confusion on the children's faces that made him feel like giving up the bike and slithering under cars until he found his Saturn, which he would easily be able to identify by its smooth tires and the rusty bolts perpetually holding his bike rack to the frame.

It was the children he didn't want to hurt, offend, penetrate like some wanton virus planting feverish images into their memories of scary grownups out of control, mild avuncular men transformed into ogres monstrous and cruel, kidnappers without conscience, child beaters. He didn't want to scare the children. But when those damned trailer hitches and aimless cars sabotaged by cell phone-addicted drivers made mockery of his equilibrium, he simply couldn't contain himself. "Fucking goddamn asshole," he'd bellow at driver, vehicle, or trailer hitch indiscriminately, as if each were equally capable of shame and remorse. And each time he tainted the air of that garage with his vituperation, he'd immediately grit his teeth and bury his head into a hunched shoulder as the good grownups, the parents the nannies the aunties, would rush to shield the ears of their children and frantically whisper prophylactic words of comfort in their tender faces, turning occasionally to throw malevolent glares at the retreating old prick.

But of all the fears that buzzed around him on this August afternoon of heavy clouds and oppressive humidity, of sweat and foreboding and melancholy, what really got to the raw edges of his nerves was the damnable garage that he was wending his way through. It was one of those enormous parking structures not dotting the city but dominating whole sections of it, block after block, everywhere you looked, rising half as high as the tall office buildings they surrounded. At least this was the way Jerry Hempstead perceived it.

And in fact it was a tall structure, twelve stories. And massive, with four ramps on each level. Two going up, two down. At times the two inner ramps would go up, the outer ones down, and then, abruptly, things would change: an inner one would stop at a chained off dead end and the other inner one would swing around to an outer ascent for a level or two, joining an inner one that would now ascend also but turn to the right instead of the left, where the lower inner ones went—left instead of right—before leading to the two exits, one at each end of the ground level. But Jerry would worry about exiting later. Right now he needed to find his Saturn.

He knew that it was somewhere near the top of the garage because when he parked it sometime around nine-thirty that morning every space on the lower levels was taken. He seemed to recall horns blaring at him as he inched the Saturn along for what seemed a half hour of searching for a hole between parked vehicles big enough for him to squeeze into. And he thought he remembered seeing a patch of overhead sky when he got on his bike to begin his long ride to wherever he went today. His current problem, however, was that in following an upward inner ramp he'd sometimes find himself, after the inner took him to an outer ramp still ascending, suddenly coasting back down a different inner ramp that was marked "All Traffic/Park" by an overhead sign, distinguishing itself from another sign that read "All Traffic/Exit," also above a descending ramp, giving him and all the other hapless drivers and riders an apparent choice more limited than the frightening "All Traffic/Park/Exit," which one of the upward ramps advised. At least with his bike he could, when he saw a sign designating a floor lower than one that he had already ridden on, such as three instead of four, walk the bike through the narrow midlevel pedestrian spaces and start uphill again; but whenever he did that it seemed to him that he was beginning the entire misadventure anew, only panting and frustrated rather than full of hope and expectation.

And, moreover, without full hope and with diminishing expectations of finding his car before suppertime so he could at least give Janna a call—he was accustomed to leave his cell phone in the car when taking his bike rides around downtown on his errands because he didn't want any distractions while maneuvering through the dense, treacherous traffic—to tell her he'd be late. Oh, how he hated to be late for her suppers, always so thoughtfully prepared and often so surprising and delicious, so much better than his, though he tried harder, at least he thought he did. But he still always used cookbooks whereas Janna just knew, just knew how much fresh herbs to use in her sauces provençal and ginger chutney and all the rest, and she knew just which courses to dress them with, to define them, to grace them, oh the salmon, oh the crab cakes, oh oh oh. What pleasure Janna had given him in his time with her—what? thirty-five years now. Thirty-five years. The playtime in bed, romping on the beach, the smell of tanning skin, taste of sweat beads, frolicking at their little summer cottage, the dining, the conversation, the patience. The patience. The toleration. Oh God, the tolerance.

That's precisely what he needed now: tolerance, toleration, and oh calm, oh for some calmness in this mad brew of a parking garage, this gumbo of anonymous pedestrians getting in his way and on his nerves and of huge trucks and SUVs and little hidden compacts backing out unexpectedly from between twenty-two foot long Dodge Rams and twenty-one foot long Chevy Suburbans, this boiling stew of walking and dashing and defiant flesh and the invincible steel and the implacable concrete that wound in rigidly directed alleys to who knows where. And he, the fly in this concoction, this dark chaos, wending his way with eternal pin pricks in his back from whatever unknowable source and with his breathless agitation, he, Jerry Hempstead, possessor of a bike and a name and a forgotten recent history—save for the image of that lovely young woman in the grass outside the ramp, the woman with amber hair, he remembered, wavy like a string of soft willow leaves floating in a northwoods stream—he, bedazzled by fear and unconnectedness, he kept pedaling, reading the overhead signs, dodging vehicles parked and moving and people cautious spirited and purposeful, wondering what this was all leading him to and away from.

The one thing Jerry thought he knew for certain was that his car was near the top of the ramp, not in the open air under the cloudy sky but near it, on the upward ramp leading to it, he thought, somewhere up there. At least he thought he knew that for sure.

He looked up and saw a sign saying "All Traffic/Park" with one arrow pointing to the right and another to the left. He chose the left and headed downward and thought, "Shit, you've got to go downward to go up," and then, realizing the absurdity of that prescription, he stopped to collect himself, a mistake on top of the directional one as it turned out, since now the whole urban parking ramp cacophony amalgamated in his head, the shouts and squeals and roars, the wind slicing across the hard low ceilings, the blasting hip hop from a dozen open-windowed cars all sounding uniformly menacing, and the incessantly pounding basses, the piercing car horns. As he stood there awkwardly straddling his bike these sounds seemed to reach a crescendo and then stop abruptly without so much as a final clang, he felt the inside of his chest thump hard several times before all functions seemed to vanish, he became aware of his ears ringing briefly in an eerie silence, he felt face to face with death. And then he heard the rumble. Or rather he heard and felt it both, it throttled him, it deboned him, it sucked him empty and then it filled him to stretching with a noxious gas. And of course he saw it all the while.

It loomed there, straight ahead. At the far end of the ramp he was descending, occupying almost the entire width of the passage: the ugliest and largest thing—vehicle?—that he'd seen in any enclosed space, a bright yellow monstrosity with black trim, its enormous wheels raising its wide slab of a body several feet off the ground, its squat flat top almost touching the concrete ceiling. The thing glared at him with hard beams of yellow and red light. The body was massive but its wide front end seemed abnormally thin, a black, grimacing, contemptuous mouth. Almost hiding the mouth was a rack of connected vertical bars, black too, three feet in height, thrust out a foot from the mouth. The windshield was low, shaded, glowering. The thing rumbled and trembled. Jerry Hempstead thought it was going to jump on him and kill him.

It seemed to want to stare him down, but it was impatient. It made the first move. With a pealing squawk it leaped forth, stopped in its tracks, stood there and shook. Startled, Jerry lost control of his stance and fell, his left leg caught beneath the bike frame, the pedal digging into his calf. He mewled and fought free of the bike, kicking it away and scrambling up. He tried to run but the injured leg buckled and he fell, yet he couldn't slow down, he scuttled along on his hands and one foot and then stopped. He turned, crouched, and tried to gauge the monster's preparedness to kill him, he glanced at the bike, now five yards away, looked up quickly and flung himself forward to the bike. Forgetting his leg he raised himself and the bike and turned and ran limping uphill.

He turned a corner and continued up an outer runway past two inner ones, one coming up to join the ramp he was on and the other going down. His intention was to stay along the periphery of the structure, away from the darker inner part, because his terror demanded it. The inner part was the bowels, and who could know what kinds of monsters, fiends, demons organic or mechanical or technological might materialize there? Out of nothing. Like the mustard-yellow thing did.

Running wobbly to avoid the revolving pedals, Jerry nevertheless managed to meet one with his shin every ten or twelve strides, and he knew without thinking that his legs were going to bleed, but he ignored the pain and the gashes as he approached and turned the next corner where he slowed to a breathless walk and finally a halt. "Holy Jesus Christ," he muttered. His head jerked and swiveled, his eyes darted madly, they began to recognize things again—parked vehicles, dank gloomy concrete, distant human forms, but not the yellow beast. Thank God, not the ugly yellow monstrosity. "Holy Christ," he said again. "I never saw anything like that."

"Holy fucking shit," Jerry Hempstead said.

Now the injuries struck. He felt the throbbing of the twisted knee, which sent sudden shocks of pain surging through him with even the slightest turn or extension, ending in an entirely involuntary gasp or yelp. He hobbled slowly ahead, saw a car back out of a space along the outer wall, heard a rap song through the closed windows. The young driver turned and looked at him, smirked, and pulled away. Jerry entered the space and stood his bike against the chest high concrete wall. He sagged against it, bent down and clutched his knees and grimaced.

What the hell was that all about, the son of a bitch, he wondered. He gripped the sore knee with both hands and shimmied it, his jaws clenched, cursing the yellow thing and the macho driver son of a bitch, cursing the lot of those SUVs and all the drivers of them everywhere, lumping them all together, hating them all. He lifted his pantleg and saw the rivulets of blood coursing down to his socks, absorbed by them, he inspected the gashes and scrapes from the steel end of the bike pedal. Great, he thought. A real gimp. Left knee shot and right leg hurting like hell and bleeding. He lowered the pantleg and pressed it against the bloody sores and he knew he was done riding the bike. Still bent but looking up, he scanned the garage for a sign of the yellow thing, the ugly fucking thing, the evil vicious deadly pernicious butt-ugly fucking no-good ugly son of a bitch. Jesus! He sprang up straight and raised his arm and pounded the top of the wall with the meaty edge of his fist. It didn't hurt as much as his legs, but the energy expended and the venom released calmed him down, and he rested against the wall and lowered his head.

He thought he heard the beast rumble somewhere, but he couldn't be sure. The other sounds of the garage resumed, and gradually he became aware of the urban noise outside the structure, buses and trucks, pile drivers and heavy construction machinery, beyond the park below and across the wide green river flowing through downtown. And gradually, too, other sensations returned.

The prickles on his back, for instance. The burning pricks. Where'd they come from anyway? Why were they there? Jerry tried, but he simply couldn't put them in perspective. Addled, he tried to think if the search for a remedy was what had led him downtown today, bike on the back of his car, parking in this godawful den of tormented confusion, not to mention contusion, God! He couldn't remember. His mind was going, he knew it, he acknowledged it, it was another thing to be scared of, racked by. It's going, he nodded. Well, that's okay if it's going. He didn't know if he particularly wanted it anymore anyway, not at all. Though Janna might be disappointed. Too much clutter anyway. Too much.

But Jesus, where did that plaguing pain in his back come from, he wondered again. Had he been attacked by a colony of mad wasps? Had he spent the last few hours with a sadistic acupuncturist? A needle wielding whore? No no, not a whore, he thought. That's not even funny. Not a whore. Never a whore. Though the afternoon's activities remained a mystery to his fear and pain fogged mind, he knew it couldn't have been a whore, needle bearing or otherwise. He'd never been to a whore, ever; never ever ran around on Janna, never ever betrayed her, with a whore or anybody else. God, he wanted to get home, at least call her. Get to his car and give her a call, let her know he's on his way, let her know he's looking forward to dinner. Have her tend to his bruises, kiss his kneecap, soothe his disturbed and terrified spirit.

The pain in his maimed legs carrying only so much command of his attention, he gave in to the need to scratch his back, reaching over his shoulders and down the neck of his shirt, around his waist, his back firm and lean and hard—because Janna liked it that way, liked his body well conditioned, robust—but unrelenting, unyielding to relief. On the back of his shoulders and on his trapezi he thought he felt a raised map of welts, and his perplexity grew. "How the hell'd they get there?" he wondered aloud.

As he scratched he felt the world becoming increasingly alien to him, something not slipping away so much as oozing in on him, slowly engulfing him, ingesting him. There were the prickles, the bleeding leg, the wrenched knee, the hurt, there was the loss of recent memory, the loss of his car, the noises, the noises. The nonsensical winding paths, meandering ramps ascending and crossing, ending and descending meaninglessly, absurdly, the crazy signs that laughed at his confusion, the outrageously excessive vehicles big enough to hold a cotillion in, and always the noise. And the noise of all noises, the noise that rose above all the others in Jerry's ears, the noise that made all the others mere squeaks in comparison: the rumble of the mustard yellow monstrosity. It rose at terror-laden intervals sometimes from a distance and sometimes too close, though never in his field of vision. Occasionally Jerry would hear the rumble followed by a screech and roar, then maybe a raised human voice cursing and echoing. But regardless of its distance, each time he heard it he felt as though it were eating him whole, shell, entrails, soul, spirit, the whole shebang. He had never felt so frightened.

And then there were the cars. As he searched for the ugly yellow thing, he began to focus on the cars parked on the ramp going up, the one he was on, and for a moment he became pleasantly distracted in this alien world he had entered. There were few trucks or SUVs on this level, almost every vehicle was a car, and they were almost all black. Almost forgetting his discomfort, he left his bike propped against the wall and wandered out from the parking space mouth agape. A '51 Mercury, black, low, with rear fender skirts. A '52 Hudson Hornet, long, heavy, a visor over the windshield. An old Nash, a big-toothed '52 Buick. All of them black and chrome, lots of chrome. The Twilight Zone, he thought. "I've entered the fucking twilight zone." A '50 Packard. A big gleaming '53 Cadillac Coupe d'Ville. A '50 Ford two-door. A Wasp. A Crosley. A Studebaker! By God, a beautiful old bullet-grilled Studebaker. What a delight, he thought. How marvelous. How totally unexpected.

How bizarre. He turned the corner and found the adjacent ramp to continue the ascent. More old cars lined the sides: black Chryslers and DeSotos and a little green Henry J. All cars from his childhood, he remembered them on the streets, his own father had a new car every other year, always Fords, never black. "Dad, why can't we get a Hudson?" he'd ask. "Or a big old Buick? Why not, Dad?" He got them through his company, had to accept what his company gave him, was the explanation. Jerry shrugged, smiled at the memory, plodded along. He heard the rumble again from a distance but paid it little mind, hobbled along. A young couple appeared, walking briskly. They divided at the rear of a nearby '49 Chevy, each moving to a door. The young man, dressed in jeans and a sport coat, inserted his key into the lock.

"Excuse me," Jerry said, approaching him. The man looked up. The woman, on the other side of the car, couldn't be seen over the roof.

"What's going on?" Jerry asked. "This is fantastic. All these cars." He extended his arm to envelop the scene. "They're all from my childhood. What's going on?"

"A vintage show," the young man said.

"Is that so?" A pang shot from his knee to his head and he winced, he came out of it with his best effort at an ingratiating smile. "So what's with them all parked here? The show's not here in this garage."

The man rested his elbow on the rear view mirror. From the other side the young woman appeared, her hair in a pony tail, wearing bobby socks and saddle shoes fifties style. "There was a big luncheon and convention at the Ravens Club across the street. In a little while there's going to be a blessing of the cars and then a parade around town." The young woman smiled innocuously and nodded, acting a role.

"Great," Jerry said. "I'll be watching for it. I've got a Saturn somewhere in this huge cavern. Used to have a navy blue '51 Ford. I liked that a whole lot better than my Saturn." Offering a little wave of his hand, Jerry wished them well and looked this way and that vacuously, as if waiting for some force to pull him either up toward his car or back down the ramp to get his bike.

With a slight shrug, he limped carefully back down, a one man procession passing the cars of his childhood. As he turned a corner to his left, he heard a throaty rumble and to his right caught sight of a mustard yellow blur two ramps over and he closed his eyes, wincing. Christ, I've got to get out of here, he thought. He picked up his pace, yelping now and then as his knee twisted or stretched, and he found his bike and felt some relief with its familiarity.

I can't ride it, he thought. What the hell. I'll either have to walk it up with this knee or leave it here and find my car and come back and find it again. "Oh Jesus," he suddenly spat aloud. Three ramps over his nemesis flashed by, the ugly yellow a streak in the dim gray of the garage. This time he heard no sound, no ominous rumble, no screeches of thick rubber on concrete. Just a flash of yellow going fast and then out of sight. God, he hated that thing. God, he hated the driver too. He hated him with a hate that drilled deep into rock, into bedrock and out the other side. He trembled with hatred. I've got to control myself, he thought, then pledged, "I will control myself."

He turned and looked outside the ramp, leaned against the chest high wall and peered at the cityscape, the gray steel and glass buildings, the concrete parking garages, the fog shrouded hills far distant. All around rain threatened, down below on the park lawn a few people waited for it, among them the young woman with the amber hair he had seen as he rode up to the garage. She sat there, seven stories down, holding a legal pad, seemingly oblivious to the breeze and impending rain.

So appropriate, the rain, Jerry Hempstead thought. Maybe it'll wash my head clean. Flush out the clutter. Let me remember stuff. Like what the hell I've been doing. Where the hell my car is. Funny, he remembered the vintage cars back in the days, remembered riding in some of them, his friends' parents' cars, even his buddies' cars when they got old enough to drive. Butch with his old two-tone blue Pontiac—navy and periwinkle? Bill's '55 Chevy held together with tape. But he couldn't remember his and Janna's first car, damn! A Ford Falcon? Comet? Something like that. God. The clutter. Too much. Too much clutter.

Confiteor Deo omnipotente…

His head lurched, a tiny but noticeable movement, a violent tic; his eyes, in his astonishment, dilated almost to bursting. These words. Where did they come from all of a sudden? These words, these Latin words long sunken, "Almighty God," these strange words, absurd and unbidden, more clutter from the distant past, like those old cars, more of the trash and detritus sweeping past the important submerged details of yesterday and earlier today in a flood of nonsense—these words: Where the hell did they come from? The old Latin altar boy prayer, Jerry wondered if any more was there.

Confiteor Deo omnipotente, his mind repeated, and he remembered what the statement meant: "I confess to Almighty God." Then the rest of the prayer jumped forth: *beatae Mariae semper Virgini, beato Michaeli Archangelo, beato Joanni Baptista* ... "Holy cow," he said aloud. "All those blesseds." ...*sanctis Apostolis Petro et Paulo, omnibus sanctis*... And the saints too, all of them.

Jerry snickered, now caught in the flow of this unexpected but increasingly engaging event. "This is amazing," he said aloud, as though to a confidante. He stood without movement or breath and closed his eyes, and as removed as he had felt from time during the past fifteen minutes—fifteen minutes? Is that all? He looked at his watch, nodded.—since he had entered the garage, he now felt removed from the space he occupied as well, floating in a realm of distant memory warm, secure, and self-abnegating. When he inhaled again the words returned unbidden ...*et tibi Pater: quia peccavi nimis cogitatione, verbo, et opera* ...*mea culpa, mea culpa, mea maxima culpa*... Through my fault, through my fault, through my most grievous fault.

"Wow, I am losing it," Jerry thought. "What the hell."

Gloria in excelsis Deo. The words poured through his mind. *Et in terra pax hominibus bonae voluntatis. Laudamus te. Benedici-*

mus te. Adoramus te. Glorificamus te. One hand covered his mouth and the other grasped the first. He stared at the park far below, at the girl with the amber hair sitting in the grass. *Hoc est enim Corpus meum.* For this is my Body. The words kept coming, streaming through him like blood. *Agnus Dei, qui tollis peccata mundi, Miserere nobis...dona nobis pacem.*

Behind him the massive yellow vehicle occupying much of the width of the ramp breathed heavily.

• • • •

> Francine sat by the window in the late morning sunshine, her eyes gazing at the pink fringed carnations in her cupped hands. They were the first gift of flowers she had ever received. Every so often she would look up and out the window at the sunlit street that shared with idle parkways the maculation [the word is underlined twice] of dying brittle leaves from doomed elm trees, and the humbled homes—once aristocratic but now divided into numerous shabby apartments like hers—and smile, and then return her gaze to her carnations. She did not want to put them in water; she did not want to not hold them; she wanted only to hold them with as much gentleness as their fragility demanded, as if she were holding tangible love or a small candle flame.

The young woman with the amber hair pursed her mouth and allowed her head to dance a bit as she finished reading these lines. She liked the last image, which had flowed through her pen onto the yellow sheet of paper so naturally, without even a prior moment's conscious deliberation. Yes, that's how it should be, love: if the concept were tangible it would be a small hot light, something quivering at times and still and calm at others, pretty, inviting, hot to the touch but not scorching or violent. Not a conflagration, she thought. But a steady thing, a thing that comforts.

With her free hand Cassie Feverlow pressed her thick hair back away from her damp forehead and temples, rubbed the back of her neck beneath the tumbling mane. Her headband was in the car on the seventh story of the garage behind her, as was the assortment of smaller bands she used to fashion a ponytail in the hot weather, and she hadn't felt ambitious or bothered enough to go back up and retrieve them, even if it meant a modicum of comfort in the oppressive humidity. Besides, she could feel the nearness of the rain. She looked at the dismal sky above the heavy gray concrete buildings and wondered at what height the drops were materializing and when she'd feel the first one. The hand that had brushed her hair back now patted the thick grass on which she sat, brushed along its tips as though over a living sable. She returned to her afternoon's work, written in her small, neat script partly in her favorite little café across the busy street and partly on a stone bench not far from the spot she now occupied on the soft grass.

> She was in the bedroom of an upstairs flat, sitting on an antique oak chair that begged for a sanding, and smiling. [Rephrase, she wrote in the margin.] Dressed in denim shorts and a red and orange paisley shirt with the long sleeves rolled up, plastic triangular earrings that dangled two inches below her lobes, her hair, a tarnished red, combed playfully by her chapped rake-like fingers, she ap-

peared superficially a child waiting in seclusion, after the frivolity and harmless pranks of the day, for some romantic stranger to come by, to whom she could fling away her aching virginity.

Should she change the "child" to "adolescent," or maybe "girl"? she wondered. "Child" could mean a seven-year-old. A five-year-old. But "adolescent" doesn't sound right. It's too clinical or something. "Girl?" "Young girl?" But they don't contain what she wanted to convey. "I'll figure it out later," she decided. Instead, she tried to picture her character, Francine, a pretty young thing in a Renoir painting, sitting there enraptured by flowers and by the image of her lover's gentle face swimming in the white petals, the curved fringes forming his eyebrows, the curls of his hair on the smooth forehead, the shape of his full lips.

The sun penetrated the window and blinded her, so she shaded her eyes and searched along the elm-lined street where she spotted the angular forms of two of her roommates leisurely approaching. They had been out all night in the rigid cold of late October. Where they sneaked off to ["sneaked? Why would they sneak?" she wrote in the margin] on the nights that the others slept their hard sleep Francine Taylor did not know, nor did she ever inquire; but they were night people, like cats, strangers to warmth and full of contempt, it seemed, for even rudimentary security. *And the stars were bright last night,* she thought. *No moon, and the stars were clear. Cold and clear stars.* "And I wonder what they did last night out there in the cold," she mused, squinting as if to slice the thirty yards of distance away, vaguely excited by the clandestine possibilities…

"Damn," Cassie said aloud at the sound of a drop on the page she was holding. The wet spot stood out immediately, doing its work on the blue ink, and she thought, "Well, I can't dry it." Slipping the tablet into her small maroon backpack, she looked up at the sky as if searching for more drops, or daring them to strike her small round eyes. The low dense clouds seemed to race through the small space between the overbearing office buildings and parking garages and what had been a breeze suddenly increased to a dank ominous rush.

"It's coming. You'd better get inside," a man's voice, hurled into the flow of air charging against it, advised. Trying to hold down her thrashing hair, she saw a man in a charcoal gray suit, his necktie flapping over one shoulder, struggling against the wind. She acknowledged his friendly warning with a laugh. "I'm ready for it," she answered.

As she stood and turned her hair became a scarf across her face, she uttered a cry of surprise and a laugh and used both hands to fight it back, its thick lushness always a pleasure to bury them in. She lost her balance and tottered into a granite planter filled with petunias and salvias and laughed again as she tried to right herself in the heavy blow. Finally, inside a glassed-in stairwell of the garage she let out a hearty "Ha!" and shook herself like a wet dog. "Whee!" she laughed. By the time she climbed the seven flights to the level her car was on, she expected the storm to hit with all its forced bravado—the winds and lightning, the crashes of thunder and the driving needles of rain; and by the time she paid her fee and drove outside the fury would probably be spent and all she'd have to be concerned about would be the curb deep puddles and a downed branch or two.

She began the climb with a smile revealing her bright teeth, her eyes picking up the images of cigarette butts and shreds of paper littering the concrete steps, recent gobs of spit, thick and revolting, and red spots that appeared to be bloodstains forming a dotted path from the first landing, where they were densely packed, up the stairs to the first level where they trailed away into the cavern of the ramp. As she climbed, the rain pounding on the glass made her think of an automated carwash. She stopped to force her vision through the almost opaque shield separating her from the harshness of the elements. Outside, splashes of water tossed rudely by speeding cars, delivery vans, cement trucks, soaked pedestrians too slow or too dim-witted to back away from curbs, umbrellas broke comically, recessed doorways filled up with desperate shoppers, clerks, and professionals seeking shelter. Down the street a cheap awning over a restaurant entrance tore and flapped, a man running across the broad avenue slipped and fell headlong and tumbled like a football receiver out of the way of an oncoming bus, a woman pushing a tandem stroller tried to hail unsympathetic taxis. The world goes on, doesn't it, Cassie mused.

What am I going to do with this story? she thought as she resumed her climb. She liked the beginning and the introduction and development of the other characters, Francine's lover and the other housemates. They were clear in her mind and, she thought, they were interesting. A couple of them exasperatingly eccentric, a couple with questionable backgrounds, some idealists. Quite a houseful. She liked them. Readers might like or despise them, but what did it matter? What mattered was Francine, what she does and what happens to her.

Cassie stopped on the landing between the second and third floors when a deafening crack of thunder shook her viscera and caused her to stutter step. With both hands she grasped the railing for support and panted, a twinge of chest pain lingering in her head. Was that like a heart attack? she thought. She looked outside, in no hurry to move on.

But her narrative problem returned. Okay, they're going to go fishing. They're going to catch a fish. A big red sucker or a carp. A trash fish. They're going to be fishing on a bank across the river from the American Legion property. Sunday evening when nobody's there. They'll catch the fish and cross the bridge a quarter mile downstream and take it over to the American Legion property and they'll attach it to the flag pole cable and they'll ceremoniously raise it up and salute it. One of the housemates will play Taps on the trumpet. They'll stand at salute and then pass around a bottle of Schnapps. They'll drink the whole bottle and then they'll go back across the river and camp for the night. Get arrested the next morning. Nasty.

The rain tapered off and stopped within a minute's time and the wind diminished to a breeze, the thunder crackled but further away, almost comforting now, we're spared, Cassie thought, another storm blustering through and fading meekly, almost making you want it to return. She turned and continued up the stairs. At the third level she heard a rumble different from the thunderous kind, a hollow, deep, mean sound, ominous, guttural almost, and she saw a bright yellow thing, a vehicle of some kind, but much bulkier than a normal SUV, flash by. She stopped, tried to spot it again, but it had vanished. She heard the rumble though, and then a squeal of tires and a bellowing horn. "Jesus," she said.

With both hands she bunched her hair and held it tight behind her head. She half hoped she'd see the thing again, she thought she knew what it was, what kind of thing, but she couldn't remember its name, only that it reminded her of war, of the war that was going on out there somewhere now, of the war that was always going on, somewhere. The war that prompted what she was writing about, the war that formed the framework of her present conundrum: where to place Francine in the plot. Should she make a statement and help to hoist the fish? Would she lose the sympathy of the reader if she participated like that, or should she stay in her room, her passivity and the gentleness of the carnations representing the kind of pacific nature that she, Cassie, the author, advocated as aesthetically and morally superior to the condition of war? One thing she was sure of: She didn't want Francine to get roughed up, as would likely happen if she joined the others in the demonstration. But could she deliberately compose it so that Francine would be spared the manhandling by a bunch of angry veterans and cops? Only if she manipulated the narrative arbitrarily, she concluded, instead of allowing the events to take their course. So, maybe Francine should decide not to go with the others. If she doesn't, maybe Teddy, her boyfriend, will decide to stay with her.

Absentmindedly Cassie opened a heavy metal and glass door and found herself on a ramp with a line of old automobiles, most of them black and chrome things from way before her time, and she spotted an old man limping along guiding a road bike turning a corner. She smiled. She recalled watching him approach the garage from the street, riding firmly but with a perplexed look on his face, mostly bald, his remaining hair longish and trailing like a small flag in the breeze behind him. He had gazed directly at her.

The way he had pedaled then betrayed not a hint of a gimpy leg.

She looked around. The color code for this floor was green and she thought hers was blue. Then she saw the floor number: eight. Her car was on seven. Forgetting the old man, she turned and re-entered the stairwell.

The brightness of the cars and their familiar shapes, the neat understatement of the sedans and the smooth boxiness of the SUVs, as opposed to the heavy steel bulk of the old-timers upstairs, reaffirmed to Cassie that she was back in her own time on the seventh floor, and she breathed in the familiarity while trying to remember the direction to take to her little hybrid, a gift from her parents for graduating from the small Calvinist liberal arts college they had set their hearts on her attending. Well, after only four years she satisfied them at no sacrifice of her sense of autonomy or identity; she had studied what she pleased and had no plans to make use of her degree in English. She was no better or worse a Christian than when she entered the place, and she reserved the right to expand or modify her thinking on theological or literary or moral grounds whenever she felt the need or the impetus. For now, her religious foundation fortified her deep inclination to despise war and to express her antipathy in her writing and in her actions.

Indeed, she had recently broached the idea of raising the fish at a Veterans of Foreign War facility not far from her parents' suburban home to some of her friends, with whom she was planning to move into an apartment closer to downtown. "What do you think, Donnie?" she had asked after presenting her idea. Donnie, short and delicate with black curly hair and eyes like onyx drills, Cassie's casual lover and closest male friend, a fellow graduate who drove a taxi, lowered his head, pursed his full lips, and winced.

"I don't know, Cassie," he said. "They did that kind of thing thirty-five years ago. I don't think it'd be too, um, safe."

"Of course it wouldn't be safe. Of course not. I mean, making a statement isn't always safe, you know."

Donnie raised his head and his eyes swerved upward. "What I mean is, there's not much sympathy out there, Cass. You do the thing, you get beaten up, the press doesn't care and you get a two-inch item on page nine B. No TV coverage probably. Your statement's not heard, you know what I mean? The media don't give a damn. They got the big celebrity killers and diddlers of little boys. They got that guy who killed his wife and three babies. So what the hell? What do they give a shit about a few throwback protesters trying to make a statement?"

Okay, Donnie, she thought, a shot of adrenalin suddenly coursing through her chest. Okay, if we don't do anything, I'll write it. I'll write it and people will see it. Some time or other, some way or other, people will see it.

She was standing on an up ramp, ascending to her left, so she turned to her right to begin the descent that would take her around a corner and, she hoped, to her car. When she got to it, she'd have to go up in order to begin her way down to an exit. The garage was becoming more familiar to her after some weeks of parking in it, but she still needed to pay more attention than she liked to finding her way around. At least she wasn't on any of the interior ramps, she thought, because those you never could be sure about. She casually looked through the dark recesses and noticed some strange cars of a different era, and as she stopped to focus her small green eyes on them she heard the thick, mean rumble that had jolted her just a few minutes earlier. Sure enough, there it was, the garish yellow monstrosity, slowly rolling down the adjacent ramp.

Well, if he's going down, she thought, relieved, he'll have to turn left when he reaches the end, and he won't come up this way. At least if he continues down. She thought. She shook her head, confused. Then she heard a shriek. And another, and a third.

Around the exterior wall of the stairwell, hidden from Cassie until she rushed the three strides and turned, were two children, the boy crying in terror, burrowing his head into the chest of a slightly older girl who was enveloping him and fighting back tears through the tightly squeezed eyes of her clenched face. The boy shook his flexed little arms and stamped his feet and went "haugh haugh haugh haugh" and then let out a long howl and repeated his mantra of fear it seemed unendingly. Cassie put her hands over her mouth to stifle a scream. She looked up and saw the yellow thing turn the corner and stop, seemingly taking measure of the pathetic tableau.

She approached the children and placed her hands on the girl's shoulder and the back of the boy's head and faced the panting vehicle twenty-five yards away. "Momma," the little girl called out, her eyes still shut. She opened them and saw Cassie and glued them onto her face and cried louder. Cassie crouched down and embraced them. They felt bony, fragile.

Against the shadowy forms of steel, the oppressive gray of the heavy concrete, and the gloom of the humid July air, the enormous yellow vehicle quaked. Its black trim snarling, its thick vertical bars menacing and nightmarish, its opaque, slit-like windshield glowering, it hurled at the huddled little human mass clench-teeth invective piercing and riving. Cassie looked at it. She wanted to glare, to stare defiant, to match its malevolent mien detail for detail, to offer death in her laser-narrow eyes. Then it began its approach.

The children seemed to sense her body tighten and the volume of their wailing increased and split her ears. She couldn't hear the vehicle's slow, grim approach but she felt it with awe. In a recess between the rear fender of a parked car and the concrete wall encasing the stairwell, Cassie felt confident that the little humble triumvirate were safe, but her trepidation consumed her. When it was within eight feet it stopped. Crouched, she realized that the thing's front end began at the height of her shoulders, the top of the little boy's head, the girl's chin. Its three-foot high vertical bars, spaced a foot apart across the breadth of the vehicle and projecting a foot and a half out from the body, looked like a bike rack for Harley-Davidsons. The boy stamped his feet and drilled his head into the girl's chest, howling his "hough hough hough" with the eerie regularity of a pile driver and the girl screamed for her mother while Cassie, furious terrified and stupefied, tried to penetrate the shaded windows in order to eviscerate the driver with her hatred. She could not see him. She had to settle for hating the machine.

And then it began to move. The tires, in height and width of tread larger than the little girl, rolled by within two yards of where they huddled. From her crouch, Cassie craned her neck to see the top of the wheel well. She followed it as it passed, saw American flag decals on the rear window, a bumper sticker reading "Support the troops." Another sticker on the center of the black covered spare wheel with the words "The Power of Pride." It rumbled away slowly, then accelerated with a squeal and turned the corner. She watched for signs of it on the distant outside ramp but it seemed to have disappeared entirely, maybe, Cassie hoped, from existence itself.

"There there, kids," she said, her fingers gently massaging the boy's soft hair, the girl's bony shoulders. "There there. It's gone now. You're okay, you're okay. Everything's okay now."

Slowly they calmed down and the normal sounds of the garage, of the city, resumed: the horns and buses outside, distant church bells, slamming car doors, reverberant stereo basses and the tough urban anger of black poets. These sounds swelled around the snivels and moans and sobs of the children, and in those intimate timeless moments of felt survival, the ineffable sense that violent death breathed on you and somehow passed you by, they wrapped all three with a panoply of solace. Life was beating again, time resuming.

"Can you tell me where your mommy is?" Cassie asked.

The girl, about eye level, tried to see her through eyes submerged in tears. The boy slowly retrieved his head from the girl's chest but didn't raise it or turn. With his head still crooked he tried to peek at the lady embracing him.

"She went to get the car," the little girl said.

"She left you here?"

"She said she'd be right back."

The boy picked up the pace and volume of his whimpering, and the girl hugged him more tightly.

Slowly Cassie learned what she had expected, that they were brother and sister, they had been warned to stay put, their mother didn't want to parade with them up and down ramps if she had a hard time locating the family car. She nodded with each minor revelation as though it were a cliché. "Well, I'll stay with you until she gets here," she said. "Let's all be calm together."

"That thing," the little boy said, then sobbed and went silent.

"Yes?" Cassie asked.

The silence endured for a moment. "It's the devil," he squeaked.

• • • •

Shambling up the ramp to the tenth floor, the vintage cars of his youth a floor or two behind and his own car soon to be found, he expected, Jerry Hempstead cursed his sore knee. He could see from his stained beige slacks that the right shin still bled, but it was the knee that prevented him from clambering onto his bike. He thought he might be able to pedal on a flat surface, but the ramp, though not steep, provided enough of a slope to make him unwilling to even try it. So he plodded on, cursing his knee and his loss of memory and, especially, the garish yellow monstrosity and its human fuckhead of a driver that brought about this latest misery, this gimpy leg, on top of his unbearably distressed back.

A respectable man in appearance, habits, reputation and, normally, vocabulary, and highly esteemed at the independent bookstore he managed, Jerry nevertheless had never given up his enormous capacity for profanity. In the privacy of his mind, in fact, he never even tried to chip away at it. His reserve of malediction was a forest thick with mottled leaves waiting in his perpetually autumnal disposition to fall and cover the earth, piling up a foundation to his life ever rotting and ever renewing. In his present discomfort his mind, mired in the sludge of his own childhood brought about by the Latin prayers so unaccountably resurrected minutes earlier, images flashed forth of parents screaming in whiskey tainted emanations the most deadly execrations in the vilest of words. These words had resounded in his adolescent head and charged back out into the schoolyards and alleys of his youth, found open expression among his streetwise friends, for some of whom—him foremost—the word "fuck" may have been the staple of their vocabulary, used a half dozen times in a typical sentence. Throughout his adult years, in a social life pretty much scheduled by Janna and in jobs ranging from secondary school teaching to his most recent position, which was now lost to him like so many other details of the last couple of days, including the accursed source of his back irritation, he had had to stifle the public expression of his depthless bile. But in the privacy of his capacious head or when he deluded himself into thinking that no one was around to hear him, his foul rain blanketed the ground of his being and drowned all hope.

"Fucking god damn thing. Ought to be fucking blown up," he told himself. "God damn thing."

"Yeah. What the fuck," he answered. "Well just keep going. Sooner or later you'll find that fucking monstrosity and that motherfucking horse's ass who's driving it will croak in his own fucking macho fucking bullshit."

"God damn leg hurts like fucking hell. Jesus Christ, I hate that SUV son of a bitch."

"Why don't you just shut the fuck up and find that god damn car and get the hell out of here."

A lifetime of such dialogue had led him to seek a wife and work and friends that would get him away from himself, allow him to balance his rage with a cultivated sanity to which he had devoted himself. You can't go on eating yourself up with hatred and profanity forever, he had realized back in his upper teens. There's got to be something more.

So when he met Janna at the junior college they attended and he fell for her beauty and kindness and the wonderfully expansive calmness she enjoyed by being who she was, a playful sprite, smart and courteous and unafraid, he gravely made a commitment to win her over and to dedicate his life to making her happy. He whispered Latin phrases in her ear (*Domine non sum dignus, ut inters sub tectum meum: sed tantum dic verbo, et sanabitur anima mea*) and she'd laugh and laugh, and he'd whisper whole poems in her ear ("She walks in beauty like the night/Of cloudless climes and starry skies…") and her eyes would moisten and she'd kiss and kiss, and he knew he wanted nothing more in life. And oh, how he wanted to get back to her now, back to her smoked mackerel and her ginger duck and her spiced apple sorbet to clean his mouth and his mind and to make him forget the godawful burning prickles in his back.

And to loll in the music of her lilting contralto as she hummed her classics, *The Poet and Peasant Overture, Tales of Hoffmann*, Schubert's *Ave Maria*, the sounds that he grew to like because she possessed them deep down in her kindness, because she gave them to him in exchange for his whispered poetry, his Latin *Missa*. So gorgeous. So meaningful.

So antithetical to the raucous assault he had been enduring for the last twenty minutes or so—it seemed forever—in this accursed inferno of a parking garage. This clanging discord, this bedlam, this bellowing tumult. He recalled the crazy noises that filled his head as he entered a swoon over a gushing injury in his youth, a severed small artery in his hand copiously mingling blood with the icy water he poured over it: the blaring and crashing brass horns blasting furiously like insane waves in his head until, abruptly, he was awakened ten minutes later, he was told, by his co-workers who had stanched the wound with thick towels and were carrying him to a car on the way to a hospital emergency room. Weird, he thought, how he could remember that incident and those noises but he couldn't for the life of him recall what he did that day. Or the last few days, for that matter.

Except the monster. He remembered the monster. Ugly fucking thing. It had caused this labored walk of his, this knee that detonated pain through his whole system every ten steps or so, and this extension on his search for his car. He should have been there by now, secured the bike onto the rack, and been out of the garage. Fuck, he spat. For all he knew, the monster—its official sobriquet now, and the name by which he would know every vehicle that even resembled it from this point forward, he decided—was the cause of the screeching cries he had heard a few minutes earlier from somewhere down in the bowels of this place, he couldn't tell where, but God they were loud. And distressed. Distinctly children's cries. He could think of no other source of that kind of terrorized wail than something purely evil, and the only thing of pure evil he could think of was the yellow thing, the thing the color of a newborn's fresh shit. Evil, he thought. Evil fucking thing. Shaking his head he let out a wet growl, loud enough to turn the heads of a couple of young men standing by their open car door. Vehicles passed him on the ramps as he walked, pulled out of and into parking spaces, people clambered in and out, strode to the stairwells and elevators with briefcases and purses, and somewhere on one of these levels the monster rolled by, or crouched and fumed, taking up an inordinate amount of space, ominous, ugly, just waiting to bully somebody new. Some children. A mother and baby. A guy on a bike.

On Level Eleven he stopped abruptly and looked out over the gray wash of the city. The Latin was returning again. As an altar boy forty-some years ago he served Mass so frequently that he remembered both his lines and the priest's, and passages he hadn't heard or thought of since quitting his service revisited him unbidden as ghosts.

Judica me, Deus, et discerne causam meam de gente non sancta: ab homine iniquo et doloso erue me. Give judgment for me, O God, and decide my cause against an unholy people: from unjust and deceitful men deliver me.

Where'd that come from? He wondered.

Quia tu es, Deus, fortitude mea: quare me repulisti, et quare tristis incedo, dum affligit me inimicus? For thou, O God, art my strength: why hast thou forsaken me? And why do I go about in sadness, while the enemy afflicts me?

He rested his arms on the chest-high concrete wall at the edge of the ramp and bowed his head low for a moment, then raised it and, surveying the cityscape before him, whispered quite audibly, "Where the hell is this God anyway?" Jesus! he muttered.

He didn't see God, he saw buildings. Some great towering steel and tinted-glass buildings, mostly gray concrete buildings from the thirties and forties of the last century, late art deco, aged terra cotta facades, no public plazas, down below a patch of a park with a few benches and some flower beds and planters, lush unmowed grass, a few young hickory trees scattered about, not much in the way of beauty, just a few feeble urban tokens. As bereft of beauty as he was of recent memory. Gray, wet, dismal. Vapid.

The rumble that was now quite familiar to him emerged in his hearing from a distance and his heart raced. Without turning around, without moving, his whole concentration fastened onto the sound, the image of the thing clearly in his mind's strong vision, the sound winding through the ramps a level below where he was standing, growing louder and receding as it followed the maze, he could trace its path, and he knew it was going to be at his level soon and then it would be behind him. His heart pounded and his adrenalin shot through him, making him a bit light headed. When it was sixty feet behind him it stopped.

Jerry pictured it there, the enormous body vibrating, snickering at him. He refused to turn around, but the image in his head would not dissolve. Then he jumped. It wasn't a high jump but it was enough to make him forget his pains and the prickling in his back, enough to make him brush hard against his bike and knock it over, an involuntary jump brought on by a horn so loud it could warn an armada of ships for miles around of its presence. An air horn, the kind used in boats on open water. "The son of a bitch," Jerry said aloud. "The fucking son of a bitch."

His chest was the thing that hurt now. Was he having a heart attack on top of everything else, he wondered. Well, what the hell, he thought. If he was having one, and if his time was up, then fuck it, it made no difference now, he thought But he refused to turn around, to acknowledge the thing, even as he heard it approach and stop feet away, only his body's length, he surmised, that close, he could smell its engine oil, its lubricants, its putrid exhaust. It stood there quivering with its restrained power and then it moved away slowly, slowly, taking its mean rumble with it, up the ramp and away.

Slowly Jerry folded his arms on the wall and lowered his head onto them. Where the hell are the cops, he asked himself. God, he'd been in this place twenty, twenty-five minutes and that thing's been menacing him and everyone else in the place for at least that long. Where the hell's security? There's got to be some kind of security around here.

All these people running around this evil-riddled place and no one calls security? No cops? No God? No one to deliver him from this evil? He limped along again, figuring on only one more level, the top one, under the open sky. He can make it, he thought. He'd be in his car soon and out of this Godforsaken hell and on the way home to Janna. She'd deliver him from this evil, he thought. This leg pain. This unbearable back If anyone can, Janna can.

She did it once before, a long time ago, a lifetime ago: she delivered him from himself, she saved his life. She opened the door with her sweet kindness and her generous body, those shapely arms and those long long legs, God those legs, and he walked through and knew that in the sacred grotto of her love was where he wanted to be forever. And it worked. She saved him, as she'd save him again from this new evil, the first evil in his memory since his own accursed youth forty-some years ago.

Sed libera nos a malo.

The words popped into his head like an ad jingle. Deliver us from evil. From The Lord's Prayer.

Aquinas said...Aquinas? He thought Aquinas? It was almost four decades ago that he learned about Aquinas. Back in high school theology class. At the time when he, Jerry, had just begun to care about such things as God and evil and sin. A short-lived time of trying to figure things out, get his life a bit straightened out. So what did he say? Aquinas. The pause to recall was brief.

He said God didn't create evil, Jerry remembered. That the notion of a perfect God creating evil was against God's nature and thus was a contradiction, and contradictions are impossible. He stopped in his tracks and his eyebrows shot upward as if in awe of the idea. So God made the world and human beings as good, he thought. Yes. And an aspect of our good nature was freedom, in imitation of God's own nature, yes, but imperfect, and so in exercising our freedom we sometimes choose actions that are called evil and that's the source of evil. Wow, he exclaimed.

All that high school theology is still in there, Jerry thought. He was making progress now, trudging up the ramp without focusing on his legs, though he limped and occasionally grimaced when the knee pounded on his consciousness. So evil is a privation of good. Great. *Sed libera nos a malo*. Deliver us from the privation. Of Good.

"But what about that ugly yellow motherfucker?" he said aloud. That son of a bitch sure qualifies as a thing, real as hell. Not a privation at all. Then a new thought entered his head and he stopped again, his eyes intense, glaring. Isaiah had God say that he, God, created light and darkness, good and evil. So that shoots down Aquinas, right? And that's Scripture. Aquinas was only a theologian.

"Shit," he muttered, resuming his labored trudge.Well. Fuck. Then a broad smile lit his face, the first since before he entered the garage. "Well," he thought, "I guess I'd rather believe a sober well-fed philosopher that a heat addled old desert prophet any day. Hah!"

But still there's the thing, and that's not a privation, he repeated. The good humor that accompanied Jerry Hempstead's brief flight of thoughtfulness vanished at the revived image of the yellow vehicle, that anti-privation, that vile excess, replaced by the fear and alarm with which he had entered the garage and which had intensified upon his encounters with it, especially this last one, the one that almost caused his chest to implode, the one that brought him to the point of giving up in despair. For the other fears returned now too, the fears accompanying amnesia, he out and about without knowing where he had been or what he had done or why. Why...Why. Or why his back hurt so brutally. Or why he felt so empty.

When he reached his car, which should be any minute now, the first thing he would do after opening the door would be to grab the cell phone and call Janna. That at least he knew he could do. He'd call her and he'd be so glad to hear her voice and he wouldn't swear even one time and he'd ask what she was preparing for dinner. And he'd try not to cry, because he felt that he'd succumb if he didn't try hard not to. And she'd say, in that lovely middle-age contralto of hers, that she's going to make lamb with a mint hollandaise and that he should hurry because it'll be ready in an hour or so. Now if only he could find his car.

Limping up from the last sheltered level of the garage and entering the blowing drizzle of the open air, Jerry encountered a new problem: he couldn't remember parking under the sky. He was certain he hadn't driven this far, yet he hadn't spotted his car on this long way up, not even any Saturns of different colors, no Saturn at all. Had he cut into one of the interior downward ramps and driven back down X number of levels to find a space? He couldn't remember, he couldn't remember anything that he needed to, damn it!—only Latin and Aquinas and dinner entrees and old cars from fifty years ago, and it was all so confusing anyway, he thought, this God damned garage with its twelve fucking floors and its ten thousand spaces and its ugly drab lifeless concrete. And thus he built his case against the city for building this monstrosity and against the citizens of this city for filling it up so thoughtlessly and for abandoning public transportation in their efforts to assert their individuality in their own little steel and plastic four-wheeled fucking skins, his rampage not sprinkled but surging now with acrimony and profanity, his mind a flooded gutter, his spirit the detritus carried by its turbid flow.

And so the fear and desperation clamping down on Jerry Hempstead as he stood under the thick racing clouds with only his head moving, swiveling actually, searching blindly for a smallish silver car that simply wasn't there, began to squeeze the last reserves of hope from his quite useless mind. At this point he no longer thought in words, not even profanity. It was as if he stood at a precipice, knowing he could either continue to stand there indefinitely or move away backward but too paralyzed to make a decision. Beyond that, he couldn't make even the beginning of an assessment.

Incapable of thought and oblivious to sensation, he failed to notice the small blue SUV stop nearby as if to wait for him to move out of the path altogether or cross over to the other side. He didn't hear the soft horn beep a couple of times, or the woman's voice ask him what he was going to do. There was plenty of room for the vehicle to pass him, and the driver made the most of it, slowly describing as wide an arc as she could past him, then pulling into a space just beyond. Jerry's eyes followed the car until it stopped, then fastened on the spot while a door slammed and the raven haired driver came into view. She was spritely with a bony face and intense dark eyes and she rushed around to the passenger side, opened the door and said, "Get out." In a moment she stood by the rear of her car, turned, barked out, "Come on I said. Can't you see it's raining?"

A little girl, four or five years old with two black pigtails, appeared. She clutched a scrawny handmade doll. The woman turned and walked several paces, but the little girl stayed put. The woman stopped, turned, snarled, "Come on. I'm not telling you again." The little girl cried out:

"The sky's supposed to be blue. They said it was supposed to be blue."

The woman seemed startled, then her body seemed to coil tightly. "What?" The word was hurled at the girl.

The little girl stood still, holding her doll at her chest. She opened her mouth like a choir member to insure the clarity of her pronunciation. "It's supposed to be blue," she shouted. "The sun's supposed to be out and the sky's supposed to be blue. They promised. They promised."

His senses fully restored, Jerry took in a deep breath and seemed to stretch. The sun's out. The sky's blue. The words resounded in his head.

The woman leaped to the girl. She grabbed her arm and yanked her and shook her several times. "You want to be cute?" she said. "You want to be smart?" She squeezed the girl's upper arm. "You want my fist down your throat?" She yanked the arm hard and started walking again, throwing a little sidearm sneer at Jerry as she passed. "I've had enough bullshit in this place," she growled.

Jerry followed their figures as they receded down into the darkness of a covered level. His lips were parted and his eyes fixed on the diminishing forms, and he felt nothing, neither the handlebars of the bike in his grip nor the gash on his leg, not his knee or the remnant of the ache in his chest from what he had thought was a heart attack on the eleventh floor. Not even the thousand pricks in his back, though they were the first physical sensations to return when the sounds resumed. And the sounds resumed with a vengeance, the horns and booming car speakers and the bus engines twelve stories down and the pinging of wind driven rain on steel machines and hard pavement all around him. The whining engines and the screeching tires. The rumblings and the child's voice crying out "The sky's supposed to be blue, the sky's supposed to be blue. The sun's supposed to be out." And Jerry's eyes widened, and his body sagged.

The sun was out and the sky was blue. Two days before, or three was it? It was three, or maybe two. Or a week. Some days ago the sun was out and under a blue sky he stood watching Janna's casket being lowered into a long deep hole in the ground. It held three red roses he had laid on it, one for each child they wanted to have but who never came, each a hole in their lives as big and dark as this one he stood over, no children to add red roses to the casket lid, no loving children's hands to add a sorely needed touch of consolation on his sloping shoulders. He watched the rose-laden casket touch the dirt down there, and then he was led away.

Now he knew the car wouldn't be here in this enormous garage. It was gone too, wrecked with Janna. He had seen it, too, crumpled and broken. Now he remembered.

It was under a blue sky when, the morning of the funeral, he had walked outside still in his pajamas, stepped off the patio onto the cool morning grass that felt so soft on his bare feet, ambled past the late flowering bushes and the nasturtiums where the hummingbirds imbibed, and past the bird bath and the lush herb garden thick with basil and sage and parsley, cilantro and fennel and rosemary, past their scent to where the grape vines ran, back by the tool shed and the little grotto with the statue of a female sprite in an attitude of prayer. It was a lovely July morning and when he had awakened he said something to Janna and reached for her but she wasn't there to share it with him, there was nothing there at all, nothing, and he felt it was somehow his fault.

He stopped by the grape vines and laid the pruning shears and rubber gardening gloves he had been carrying gently on the ground, then took off his pajama shirt. He put on the gloves and picked up the shears and approached a section of vines guarded by wild nettle plants, the leaves of which he used for tea after having read of Buddhist recluses living on it alone. And under the sunny blue sky he cut a number of the five foot leafy stems that appeared so delicate and he bunched them up in one gloved hand and he flagellated his bare back and he cried out in the reverberant privacy of his skull for Janna, because he did not want to see her put into the ground later that morning.

Now he stood still and closed-eyed and he knew without words that he had to leave this hellish garage and force his way somewhere. He didn't know where for certain. Maybe work? The image of a neatly lined shelf of books flashed through his mind. No.

No.

Maybe home? Maybe.

• • • •

In the sane and stable space of her little hybrid car, Cassie Feverlow took in a deep breath and began a search for her water bottle. It would be quite warm now, the ice cubes having melted long ago, but she wouldn't mind, she was absolutely parched.

Rain fell outside and even in the shelter of the garage the air was so muggy it seemed to drip. Not only that, it also wrung whatever moisture remained in her body out through her pores, dampening her motley sleeveless slipover and the crotch of her denim shorts, soaking and flattening her lush hair around her face and behind her neck. She found the plastic bottle on the floor behind her seat, uncapped it, and sucked hard and deeply. As she recapped it she grimaced at its warm tastelessness, then searched for a band to tie her hair back.

Cassie loved her hair. She loved the feel of it, its rich texture, its thick abundance, its subtle amber glow. She loved its sensuousness and she loved the attention certain men—the kind that she liked, the hungry sentimentalists—paid to it, the aroused acquiescence it prompted in them, their gentle hands scooping it over their faces as if eager for the helplessness of finding themselves lost. But now, still trying for a bit of calm after the fright she shared with the children over that ugly monstrosity and that conscienceless bastard of a driver, all she wanted was to get that heavy, sodden hair away from her face and neck.

The band showed up in her glove compartment and she pulled back her hair and fashioned a tail and sighed. She stared straight ahead for a lost moment or two, then answered a call from somewhere to take a look at herself. The small rearview mirror revealed only her eyes and the narrow bridge of her nose, so she extracted a larger glass from her backpack and found her whole face in it and peered at it.

Faintly her head nodded. Yes, she thought. It can be a mother's face. As the words came forth, her face softened and a subtle smile formed. "You'll be a good mom someday, Cassie." Her eyes lowered and she felt the two frightened children in her embrace, their fear palpable, thrumming with aliveness. She looked back into the mirror. Their mother hardly deserves them, she thought. Nice as she was, she hardly deserves them for leaving them like that, even if it was for just a few minutes.

"What's happening? What's the matter?" Cassie hadn't looked up when the woman's voice rang out with alarm as the car door opened. She was still holding the kids and had turned her head and watched as the car approached and halted abruptly, but she didn't look up at the woman. She saw a heavy sandal clad foot hit the pavement and a heavy bare leg, then the other, and she slowly released the children and their dank odor and as she rose the woman sank to her knees and hugged them. Her plaid shorts seemed ready to split and beneath her thin white blouse her wide banded bra bit deeply into her back. She looked up at Cassie.

"They were frightened by that big yellow thing that's driving around here."

"That...what do you call it? That, that...what do you call it? That big thing that that son of a bitch is driving around terrorizing everybody with? Is that it?" She turned to her children. "Did that big thing scare you kids?"

They nodded vigorously. "We thought he was going to run us over," the girl said.

"Why didn't you run? You could have hidden in the stairwell."

"We were too scared," she said.

The mother said she'd get the cops here, thought Cassie. Where are they? She continued to study herself in the mirror. Do I dare pull out and try to drive away? she wondered. Should I just stay here until the cops come? She put down the mirror and lit a cigarette. "I've got time," she said aloud.

The cigarette filter clinging to her dry lips, she opened her backpack and retrieved her notebook and thumbed through the scattered notes and passages. What she was looking for, she wasn't sure of, but she felt a certain impulse to run through the pages until she found something to satisfy the urge. When she came to an exchange between her character Francine and a roommate who would be involved in raising the fish at the vet's club, she stopped and read thoughtfully.

> "You look tired, Terri."
>
> "Oh, I am, rather. Didn't get a bit of sleep again last night."
>
> "You take a nap right after lunch then, okay? You'll need rest in order to catch that prize carp this afternoon."
>
> "I don't think so, Francie," she said. "I despise sleep, you know. I'll be all right."
>
> "But you really should."
>
> "No. It's all right, it's all right. I don't like to be not conscious, you know. Unless I earn it, that is. You know what I mean, Francie?"
>
> "I...I think so. But, I don't think I understand."
>
> She followed with her eyes as Terri walked across the room and back, her hands clasped behind, a wraith in baggy jeans and worn wool shirt.
>
> "Simply because sleep is so, so ...it's such a kind of obsequiousness. That's it. It's like—helpless, you know? A kind of submission. To the facts of life, if you know what

I mean." She jabbed the air with both hands. "And I just don't like that."

"No, I don't know what you mean."

"What?"

"'The facts of life, if you know what I mean.' No, I don't know what you mean."

"Oh you know, the bullshit. The games. The work. The *relationships*. The *stuff* of everyday living. The stuff that's supposed to wear you out by the end of the day." She lit a cigarette and blew the smoke out dramatically. "I don't like to be worn out by that stuff. If I'm going to be worn out, I'm going to be worn out on my own terms."

There was a pause and then Francine said, "Isn't that odd?" In the background someone was playing the overture to *Tannhauser*. She listened a moment and continued. "And I'm just beginning to feel the opposite. Like repose is all. I'm getting to feel kind of tired of it all, Terri. Like all I want is to sit here disengaged from everything. With my carnations." She cupped them and raised them to her nose. "Because nothing will do any good. I mean, so we go this afternoon and catch a big sucker or a big carp or some goddamn big fish and tonight we raise it up the goddamn flagpole and salute it. Okay, so what good will it do? I mean, tomorrow we'll get arrested and we'll maybe get beaten up and we'll go to jail and get out eventually and nobody will care or understand what we meant, and nothing will be accomplished. See? It won't do any good."

"But listen, honey." Terri threw herself into a moldering leather chair. "You talk like that and you'll be drawing the blood out of life itself. And you know what that will mean. That means we'll be nothing, nobody will be anything, but a bunch of bones and skin with little cryptograms inside us shooting around saying things like 'Bow down now' and 'Get fucked now" and 'Say your prayers now and 'Eat your food now,' and on and on. But doing the thing that counts—that's life. That's spirit. That's what's *human*."

Francine raised her flowers to her lips. "But Terri, all the suffering."

"*That's* human."

"But the, the willingness of it."

"That's the most distinctly human." She sprang forward. "No. That's divine."

Cassie lowered the notebook and lit another cigarette, thinking "What the hell. I didn't have any for three or four hours." Then she read the last words again: "That's divine." She lowered the notebook again.

"Bull," she said.

"What a crock," she said.

Then she thought, "That was the character who said that, not me." But then she thought, "Yes, but when I wrote it, that's what I was thinking."

Why would she think such a thing, she wondered. Had she herself ever suffered, really suffered? She didn't have to consider for long. No. No suffering. A little flu now and then. Some anxiety. A couple of lost romances. Some anger, some lingering resentments. Some serious embarrassments. She smiled. The time she was caught by a fervent Calvinist roommate printing a porn image from a website in her dorm room. "Cocksureboyznbuff" was the site. God, what a hunk! That one went all the way to the dean of students via the resident advisor and the student newspaper. Now that was embarrassing. But did she suffer? No. She felt like an orange squeezed in a juicer, she recalled, that was the image she came up with herself, her emotions the juices wrung out of her reputation and her identity and sampled by everyone on campus. Well. But that humiliation didn't constitute real suffering, she recognized, because all along deep down she was snickering. And she was joined in that tacit amusement by her parents, good libertines that they were, both graduates of the same place who sold her on the quality of its programs while grinning at its denominational tilt, when she told them about the situation she was in; she could see signs of subtle chuckles on their faces when they cleared their throats and rolled their eyes. Cocksureboyznbuff, indeed, they conveyed. Go girl, they seemed to say.

So no, she hadn't ever truly suffered. So the next question was, did she know anyone else who had really suffered? The list of relatives who had died was small, and none that she knew of had endured grave illness. She had lost no friends to perdition or death, and she was aware of none with mental problems more serious that the ordinary concerns of identity and finances. Indeed, with regard to misfortune and pain, Cassie had always thought of herself as more than a little lucky. In light moments, over jovial beers with friends, she even thought she might be one of the Elect.

"Yeah, elected by Cocksureboyz," one of her friends said with his glass raised.

Cassie allowed herself some snorts of laughter at the memory, but her light mood faded as her senses recalled the trembling bodies of the two children she had embraced only minutes earlier. She wiped the moisture from her forehead and the back of her neck as she thought of them. Now there was some pretty intense fear going on, she thought. Pretty intense. They may forget it tomorrow, but when they felt it they were suffering. Alone. Small and helpless. An enormous beast looming in the gray light of the dank garage, deliberately terrifying them. Their mother nowhere in sight. Yes, that probably qualifies as suffering.

But another qualifier, she thought: Time. The real suffering of those kids was only five minutes or so in duration. Once Mommy came and soothed them, they were over it. Anyway, if they got out of the garage without running into that bastard again. God, I hope so. And I hope the mother calls the cops like she said she would. She said herself that he's been driving all over the garage scaring people. I wonder why no one else has called the cops. I wonder if he's hurt anybody. I wonder…

She slouched, leaned on the door handle, thought about another cigarette but held off the urge as the subject of her contemplation abruptly returned.

But imagine, she continued, a suffering as intense as those kids's but that goes on over time, that may recede for periods but that dominates a good part of a person's life. That may go indefinitely, maybe until death alone can end it. That kind of suffering, the suffering of the tortured political prisoner. The suffering of chronically depressed, the perpetual griever: Is that sacred? Sacred? Is it?

"Bull," she said aloud.

As though oblivious to any destination other than deeper immersion into her own reverie, Cassie got out of the car and walked over to the chest-high wall and rested her arms on it. The sky threatened more rain, maybe another storm, and the noise of the traffic below was heightened by the slick streets. "So what makes you even think of suffering as being divine?"she asked herself.

Was it Jesus? All the movies and stories of his suffering? A theology based college education? Running gore and crunching bones and flayed skin in a popular motion picture assigned for credit in her Theology 321 class. And I got in trouble for printing off Internet porn, she thought. An image of a body whole and beautiful. Gorgeous. She smiled playfully. And I got in trouble for drooling over that.

But rather than the vision of a sleek model stud forming clearly in her mind, the past hurled another image quite starkly different, quite starkly agitating: Christ's face in purple shadows, bloody drops profuse on brow and cheeks, eyes black-clotted, crusty lips broken open, blighted, crawling tongue, head lolling mechanically side to side. She woke to that hideous image one night at the age of eight, her fragile body soaking the sheets with her child's sweat, she lay there staring at it on her bedroom ceiling for the longest time, forever it seemed, before she opened her mouth to scream, and she screamed and screamed but not a sound tore out of her gaping mouth, nor did a tear fall. For a long time after that night she thought of herself as one of Jesus's special children, but she told no one and the suffering Jesus never again revisited her except occasionally, as now, in her flawed memory. She shuddered, shook her head.

Well, no doubt Jesus suffered, Cassie thought, and it was pretty intense and brutal. But it lasted only a few hours, a half a day or so. Would a baby born with full-blown AIDS who lived two years qualify as divine too, maybe more divine than Jesus? If suffering is divine, that is?

Her thoughts stopped abruptly and she felt her heart accelerate. Without turning to look she knew that the dreaded yellow vehicle was not far away. It spoke to her and to all within hearing with its dreadful rumble, its evil mocking acrimony. She was going to turn around and look for it, it would be easy to find, grisly yellow that it was, but before she made a move her heart seemed to explode and she felt her feet leave the ground for an instant and she felt harsh air forced through her throat and out her open mouth but heard not a sound, and when she landed she swirled around and saw it on the same level but two ramps over, and she saw a bald man rising from the pavement over a fallen bicycle and stand there staring the monster down. A hand held a small white thing out the window and the sound blasted again, and she involuntarily jumped again, and her heart, which hadn't yet stopped pounding, seemed to detonate again. The distant hand retracted and the dark window closed and the yellow thing backed away out of sight.

The sound of the air horn Cassie had heard maybe twenty minutes earlier while in the stairwell, but from enough of a distance that it had merely startled her. It was before her own run-in with the crazed driver of that enormous brute, the driver himself obviously a brute and more, a terrorizer of old men as well as of children. She watched as the bald man, after standing motionless for a short time, picked up his bike and walked. He was limping, she noticed, and it was a severe limp. If she stayed where she was, he'd pass her within minutes. Maybe she could ask him if she could give him a hand.

Cassie's eyes followed the old guy as he struggled down the

neighboring ramp, and it occurred to her that this event taking place, like no other in her experience, was like some movie or television melodrama, or maybe even an old morality tale spun from a resurrected English minstrel, somehow unreal and maybe even a teensy bit hackneyed, but definitely disturbing, unsettling. How nice it would be if this were a piece of fiction, she thought, the product of a cunning mind not unlike so many she had encountered in the four years spent in and out of classrooms while sheltered by ivy and guitars and people talking softly about things like semiotics and hermeneutics. Not to mention theology.

She curled her lip. Well, she had taken her theology and gotten her C's, and none of it had prepared her for this scene: This monster, this soul inside the monster, this molester of children and old men, and this fear he had generated unlike anything she had feared in her twenty-two years, this fear too real to be hackneyed, a mere product of fiction. She was suddenly aware of the digging of her fingernails into her palms; she opened her hands and peered at them and saw sweat and deep slits. She stretched her fingers wide and reached out her arms and slowly raised them flexed and tense and allowed them to fall to her head, her wide open hands pressing hard into her coarse, tight hair as she breathed deeply and repeatedly.

"Oh Christ, this has got to end," she groaned.

But it wasn't going to end. She heard the rumble again. It was down the ramp she was on and around the corner and down some more, facing upward, the wrong direction. She traced the path and saw the flat black top and the squinty shaded front windows, the blackened side windows and a broad slab of mustard yellow above the low wall separating that ramp from a dead-end interior surface.

It was not moving, only fulminating. Cassie's heart jumped and raced. "Why won't it go away?" she thought. Then, "Where are the cops?" A moment later: "Where is somebody? Anybody."

Unable to take her eyes off it, she saw the massive wheeled fortress accelerate forward slowly. It seemed to be rolling slowly up the slight incline of the down ramp and approached the corner and Cassie held her breath as it turned and faced her. When it faced her it stopped again. The black front end with its menacing rack of black bars rising upward almost three feet from the ground, the dark scowling windows, the broad squared off body and roof—the thing looked like death to her. She took in her breath jerkily and audibly and she held it, as if protecting it. She heard the motor revving.

"Is it coming after me?" she thought, tears flooding her eyes. As it resumed its slow acceleration, thirty yards away from where she was planted, she let out her breath and took in another one, beginning to resign herself to something she felt was too big for her. The thing seemed to stutter toward her, rolling, stopping, rolling, stopping. Something made her whip her head for a flash to the opposite direction, return it to the monster, and whisk it back. Her eyes focused on the bald man with the bike rounding the corner at the lower end of the ramp, thirty yards away. Maybe he can help me, she thought.

When she turned back the vehicle was only yards away and she gasped. Her hands flew to her head again, one of them slid to the back and grabbed on to her thick tail and slid halfway down and pulled tight. She grimaced as the thing approached, its menacing front rack extending, reaching out, and then it was in front of her enormous and overwhelming. She felt as small as a child as it passed before her, seemingly eternally, and then it was beyond her and she was safe but now she felt herself shaking. She saw the bumper stickers, heard them mocking her: "The Power of Pride," one read, "Support the Troops" read the other as the thing moved slowly on, she saw the flag decals, the image of a fish dangling from a flag pole invaded the picture and she felt insignificant, puny, a comic figure trembling in the muggy heat, a helpless gyrating cipher.

From somewhere the sound of sirens penetrated her mind but didn't register. Instead she heard the rumble of the yellow vehicle now ten yards past, that gnawing rumble, that rumble, that ceaseless coughing growl, and then she heard a screeching sound and she cast her attention upon it and finally distinguished incomprehensible words piercing and terrible: *ora pro nobis orapronobis orapronobisorapronobis*, and on and on, and she lost sight of the bald man hidden now behind the slowly advancing vehicle. She took two steps toward the unfolding action and halted, she heard a crashing sound and saw a bicycle fly upward from the front of the vehicle and strike a concrete bulkhead and ricochet off it onto the broad flat roof and slide off. My God, he threw it at the thing, she thought. The vehicle continued forward, slowly, and Cassie now ran down the slope and caught up to it. She was screaming now: "No. No. Stop it. Stop it," screaming alongside the impenetrable yellow steel wall on the driver's side as the vehicle continued rolling forward, and she saw the bald man limping backward, his mouth open and eyes wide and hands extended toward his enormous adversary, that inexorable and insatiable monster, and the driver of it hidden within.

Frozen again, her hands splayed on the sides of her face, Cassie cried formless sounds. She heard sirens somewhere and then heard them stop, and she saw the vehicle drive the bald man to the wall, and it seemed to her that she was seeing the scene as through the eyepiece of a camera, the bold black and yellow decaled backside of the monster heaving like a garish bull just off center against a dismal gray field framed by gray concrete. She ran a few steps forward and stopped, seeing an awful thing. It was the bald man Jerry Hempstead's head seemingly planted on the hood of the vehicle like an ornament. She saw his arms, too, extended on the hood's top with his hands lying flat. He seemed to be pressed against the waist-high wall behind him and his face was expressionless save for his eyes wide and depthless.

And then the thing began to back up. And the bald man Jerry Hempstead's head and outstretched arms came along with it.

"Hah?" Cassie cried.

She ran forward as the thing backed up. "Oh no oh no oh no!" she cried as she reached the front of the thing and saw the bald man Jerry Hempstead's body squeezed between two bars of the protruding rack, his legs forced to pace along with the vehicle's slow reverse movement. He did not look at her. His wide-open eyes were riveted ahead. "Get out, get out, get out," she screamed, her hands alternately pulling down on her ponytail as if trying to generate something, some force, some energy, something. But she could not move her legs to approach him.

"It's a but-ter-fly, Cassie. Isn't it pretty, Honey? It's called a monarch. Mah-nark. Mah-nark. Can you say mah-nark, Cassie?" Her daddy's voice, his kind, loving voice. Out of the distant past. *The butterfly, so pretty, she squatting on the fine beach sand at age two, it posing there for her, twitching its lovely black and orange wings, so*

delicate. The image never left her. Daddy bending over her, the monarch in the sand, the sun bathing them all. And then the foot. *The ugly man's-foot, long, tendony, long big knuckled toes, inches away from her little face, the slender body suddenly gone, the delicate wings suddenly broken and twisted between bony toes, toes pressing down the sand and disappearing for a moment and the heel rising, and then the whole foot rising with the twisted orange and black wings mangled and fluttering in the movement and then crushed down again, she following the foot and wondering what happened, Daddy swearing.*

Her hands seemingly charged by their violent pulling at her hair, Cassie released her tail and flung herself at the driver's door of the thing and pounded it and shrieked. "Let go of him, let go of him, you bastard. The cops are coming, you're ass is grass you son of a bitch, let go of him God damn it." Springing along sideways as the thing moved backward, her fists impervious to the hardness of the opaque windows, she pounded and cursed until the heavy door flew open as if enraged itself and bashed her arms into her face and hurled her backwards against the trunk of a parked car and down to the concrete floor.

"Fuck you, bitch," a voice boomed.

She looked up and saw a man's lithe body leap out of the vehicle and when his feet touched the pavement he turned and bounded back into it and she saw and heard the door slam and then open again.

"Fuck you, you bitch," the man yelled again and then slammed the door shut again and before she could scream a rejoinder she heard the revving of the engine and she scrambled up and stood crouched, tense. She saw the bald man Jerry Hempstead stuck between the bars his wide-eyed face still expressionless save for his sadly raised brows and she saw his hands turned up with only the middle fingers extended and then she heard a squeal of tires and the monstrous ugly thing roared forth and shot through the chest-high concrete wall with a percussion shocking and deafening and disappeared amid chunks of concrete great and small and flying like drab sparks before vanishing too.

Like a granite churchyard figure Cassie crouched, her arms spread out and bent upward, her hands cupped and motionless above her head, screaming into hoarseness. Only her screams filled her consciousness, and when they faded there was nothing in it for a time but grayness and a void. And then she moved forward in a stealthy crouch toward the broken wall with its jagged severed and bent steel rods protruding messily, her face graven with features warped and tragic. At the edge of the floor she sank from her crouch to a squat and almost lost her balance but caught and steadied herself with a hand to the pavement and she looked down and beheld the blight in the park below, the shattered pieces of mustard yellow steel and chunks of wet concrete, the broken fountain containing the grotesque bulk of the dead monster, the spume of dust rising sluggishly in the sodden air, the surging clusters of people, fire trucks, police cars. She saw no sign of the sad bald man.

Now her mind was blank and there were no more thoughts about the divinity of suffering or the raising of fish on flagpoles or the choice of repose over action meaningful or useless. What she saw and what she heard now, the pieces of color, the alarmed and aimless movement, the formless cacophony, were nothing more than swatches of sensations bouncing off the numbness of her squatting shell.

She sat down on the chunky edge of the wreckage and dangled

her legs and stared through her gathering tears. In time she saw dust particles risen from far below settle on her feet, and she wondered wordlessly at it all.

A VISIT TO THE DENTIST

How often do we like to think that what we experience is exceptional? That we are just a little more merry than others at holiday parties, that we are just a bit more appreciative of fine art or fine dining than others, that even though of a lower status than the subjects of New York Times Magazine beautiful people we are perhaps a tad more receptive to the good things of life simply because they are always so new to us, so refreshing, so exhilarating. And don't we like to think of how much more enduring we are? That is, don't we often like to consider ourselves a bit more brave than others in, for example, putting up with physical pain? How often do we compare our suffering with that of others, our anguish, our mourning, our capacity to surmount the vicissitudes of life, the misfortunes, the calamities even, the awful sorrows. Daily? Twice daily? Maybe only weekly. Well, for most of us, probably not infrequently.

And so upon glancing at him we wouldn't think twice about

labeling someone like Larry Dooney a punk, a fool, a queer, a wastoid, a nerd, a geek, or any number of other contemptuous epithets depending on our own status or disposition, though some of those words hadn't been coined yet when he left the dentist's chair and staggered out of the small office and onto Market Street back in the early nineteen sixties, squinting in the early afternoon glare of a June sun, his lips in a taut snarl and his hands clasping the sides of his head as if holding together a brittle and deeply cracked vase. It had been a long day so far, and now he had to orient himself, walk a few blocks to a bus stop, wait for who knows how long, and ride several forlorn miles to an automobile parts manufacturing plant to apply for a summer job which he probably wouldn't get and for which he felt completely inadequate. What made him such an easy mark for derision were his uncombed hair that rained white powder onto his narrow shoulders, his black horn rimmed glasses that doubled the area of his normally slitted eyes, and his springy gait. On the other hand, he was wearing new shoes. Black ones. Penny loafers. With wooden heels that scraped the sidewalk and sounded cool. So once he started walking, soothed by the cool sound of his shoes' heels, he was able to let go of his wounded head, allow the soft breeze to dry the moistness in his eyes, and admit to the feeling of exhilaration over having ended his orthodontic ordeal with a huge exclamation point, no matter the feebleness of his effort.

Having never had his teeth, much less his gums, touched by a sharp or pointed instrument in his eighteen years, possessing in fact pristine teeth and gums untouched by any hand other than his own—tongues occasionally, yes, but not fingers—he nevertheless had mentally braced himself for some pain. Over the years all his friends had described their agony during scrapings and drillings, the meanness of dentists, the callousness of their assistants; and so he had reckoned that the root canal he was to have would cost some squirms, some mute curses, maybe even some tears oozed through tightly shut eyes. But he knew pain, so he hadn't been too worried. If it got too bad, he'd simply think about the chronic shin splints that made him think his legs were going to shatter like brittle glass every day of the track and field season and through much of the summer, even now, two weeks after graduation.

Yes, he knew pain. A trip to the dentist's office, even for something as sinister sounding as a root canal, couldn't be so bad. Certainly it could be nothing like the migraines. Jesus, the migraines. They sometimes lasted three days. Three days! Oh the migraines, the nausea, the crying into soggy pillows, the constant fantasies of diving headfirst out the second story bedroom window, through the glass and all, onto the concrete driveway below. If he could stand that happening every three or four weeks, he could take anything the sissy overeducated dentist could throw at him. So late that morning, snorting, he had shoved open the heavy glass door to the storefront office with the bravado of a righteous cinematic gunslinger entering a saloon. Inside, he stood with feet wide apart and thumbs in his pantwaist surveying the room. It looked like a barber shop to him, the one down the street he had patronized since early childhood, except with slightly more modern chairs than he was used to. There was a big wall mirror, a ceramic basin standing next to each chair, a small table next to each basin with strange, sharp looking instruments laid out on their cloth covered surfaces, and a single armlike contraption descending from the ceiling. The X-ray machine, he recalled from his only other visit to the office.

Truth to tell, he had actually been to the same dentist two weeks before for the X-rays, evaluation and analysis that led to today's appointment. But he preferred to keep that secret. Some of his more credulous friends even held him in awe when he told them that his mother had simply called to schedule a root canal for his first-ever appointment. "Wow!" they cried. "You mean that this is your first time ever? That's amazing! You mean you're gonna have the big ouchie on your first visit? Man, I've gotta hand it to you." After impressing them into such a pitch of admiration, he certainly wasn't going to tell them that he had actually seen a dentist, a different one, back when he was thirteen, after his right upper front tooth had joined his immediate neighbor, which was a right triangle, in perdition by turning a dusky gray. "Dead," that early dentist had proclaimed. "It's done for."

"Are you going to take it out?" the scared pubescent Larry asked.

"You're too young for a false tooth," the dentist said cheerfully. "You don't want to be bothered with that. No, what we're going to do is wait on it. You've got some growing to do yet, so we're going to wait until you stop your growth and then we're going to shave those teeth down, both of them, and attach a cap to them. That way you won't have to put up with false teeth in the front of your mouth. I'm sure you wouldn't like that at all. Messy business."

"You mean I've got to keep these teeth looking like this?" Larry asked. He hadn't even started high school yet. He had four years of high school to look forward to. To anticipate. Now to dread. Images of gagging girls and derisively laughing boys filled his brain. He'd have to train himself not to smile. To laugh. He'd be with his friends, if he had any, and he'd have to croak back any mirth that might arise, any surprise, amazement, any joy or celebratory yelp, he'd have to stifle all his feelings, and at the end of four years he'd be elected class sourpuss, class grump, least likely to have any friends, least likely to ever have a job, least likely of any category the fresh faced and sparkly toothed graduates could concoct specifically for him to occupy. If he even finished high school. He saw himself as a junior year dropout, age sixteen, pumping gas somewhere down in central Indiana where the swine don't care what your teeth look like or even if you have any. He could pump gas with a whole haycock stuck in the triangular gap in the front of his mouth down there in central Indiana. And nobody would give a damn about the black tooth when half of them probably didn't have any front teeth at all.

"You can have a seat in that chair," a freckly young woman said to the gunslinger wannabe, pulling him out of his memories and indicating the chair to the rear of the room. "Just sit back and put your feet up here, and I'll get you in position. Doctor will be right in."

He lowered himself onto the leather covered chair and raised his legs up and, full of a young man's bravado, he relaxed, his eyes roaming the walls, lingering on pictures of gums collapsing from gingivitis and others depicting teeth brown with advanced decay. Beyond these were framed prints of grassy fields carpeted with daisies. One wall was covered with mirrors, and he caught sight of himself and grinned broadly, hoping that this would be the last time he would ever face the grotesqueness of those front teeth. The chipped one had come first, when he was twelve. A friend had surprised him by grabbing his ribs from behind, and his reaction was to double over and strike the edge of a tabletop with his mouth wide open in mid scream. The tooth hit the edge and broke cleanly. He felt as if he had been shot in the head and he burst into disconsolate crying in front of his buddies. The black one he killed ice skating on a public rink, trying to match his friends' graceful starts, stops, and loops in their shiny black figure skates with his own scuffed hockey skates. That hurt too, of course, but with the dull pain of a heavy thud rather than the shattering current of a power surge, though the distress continued for days, he recalled, like a weight on his upper gum. Probably the groan of the dying nerve, he thought. At any rate, those original discomforts were long gone, he thought now. Whatever distress he had to face now couldn't be much worse, and like them it would disappear in no time.

He finished his survey of the room as the dentist entered it, his eyes sweeping past the tray with its display of strange and forbidding tools, the upright basin next to his chair, and the adjustable arm of the lamp over his head. He sat up and turned to greet the dentist, a man in his early thirties with a bland face made somewhat interesting by the magnification of his eyes behind thick lenses.

"Good to see you, Larry," the dentist, Doctor Wehrmann, said. "You can just sit back and relax, and I'll explain what I'm going to do for you today."

"Ah, you're going to give me a train ticket to Chicago?" The question shot out impulsively and was followed by a burst of forced laughter. Doctor Wehrmann smiled tolerantly.

"Well, it won't be quite that much fun," he said. "But it'll be a lot more beneficial in the long run." His face became benign, almost saintly. Larry liked him, felt ready to place his life, if need be, in the good doctor's hands. "What I'm going to do is to begin you on your journey to a new attractiveness and a new sense of self-confidence. It'll be a two part process," he said. "The first part is this. In order to fit you with permanent caps we'll have to grind your front teeth down to stubs and we'll put some temporary caps over them until a week or two from now when your permanent ones should be here. The grinding will take about twenty-five minutes and won't be too uncomfortable." He smiled kindly. "The second part is called a root canal. By that I mean we simply extract the nerve behind this front dead tooth before it begins to deteriorate further and turn infectious. If it turns infectious, your whole gum will become infected and you'll be in real trouble because that could lead to your teeth falling out one by one. The other big problem, of course, is the nerve dying." He continued to explain what would happen if the network of nerves in his upper jaw died and rotted, and the lifelong consequences of such a catastrophe to a man so young and promising. His voice carried a mixture of warmth and professionalism sufficiently convincing that Larry Dooney fell into a love for him as profound and unreserved as his love for his father.

"I'm in your hands," said Larry Dooney.

The freckled aide tied the strings of a small bib behind his neck and invited him to settle down. He stretched out and relaxed, his fingers loosely intertwined on his belly, and he followed the lamp as it was adjusted above his face. "You said the first part will take about twenty-five minutes," he said. "How long will the second part take?"

"Oh, about a half hour. Maybe forty-five more minutes." Doctor Wehrmann wasn't smiling now. He was positioning the odd looking instrument with the small abrasive wheel at its end above

Larry's mouth, and he seemed eager to begin his work and not waste any more time chit-chatting. Pressing a pedal on the floor, he activated a pulley which started the instrument and he carefully focused in on his patient's gaping mouth.

So far it doesn't hurt, thought Larry Dooney, quite pleased with himself at not so much as flinching when the tiny burr first touched his triangular tooth. This is nothing, he thought, though he did take notice of his fingers, no longer interlaced but clenched. Well, at least his nails weren't digging into his palms, and he felt them relax after another few seconds. But he couldn't help noticing a mildly unpleasant odor accompanying the whiney buzz of the instrument, and he concentrated on studying it. Burning, he thought. Something smells like burning...like burning skin. Or hair. Burning hair. With his mouth wide open he wasn't able to grimace with disgust, so he imagined it, lips curled baring teeth and gums like a dog's mouth after chewing on a particularly putrid roadside carcass. It was an odor that both fascinated and repelled him. He had smelled it on a couple of occasions when, too close to a leaf fire or a campfire, the coarse hair on his wrists was singed off. More recently, only a month ago, his right hand and wrist were scalded by water backed up in a coffee machine at the fast food restaurant where he earned a few dollars on weekends during school. He wanted to smile as he relived the scene while the tiny wheel wore away the enamel of his half tooth:

"Hey Larry. That coffee ready yet?" Larry spun around from the window where he was setting up a tray for the curb service woman who addressed him to see, then whirled to look at the coffee maker. A good five minutes earlier he had put a clean filter into the funnel, poured in some fresh grounds, and flipped the on switch, so the pot should have been filled by now. The pot was empty. His head swung from the empty pot to the curb server on his left to the line of dinnertime customers on his right and to his colleague behind him pouring milk before returning to the coffee machine. “I know I started it,” he began as his hand swished through the narrow space of his work area and clutched and pulled the funnel out from the grooves at the machine’s top.

Without warning, as he detached the funnel the nearly boiling water that had backed up poured onto his hand and lower arm. As soon as the pain registered in his mind his arm tossed the metal funnel up to the ceiling and he screamed “Jesus Christ” and doubled over, his swelling hand couched in his abdomen and his feet performing a crazy dance in the puddle on the floor. “Shit shit shit shit,” he whimpered. His co-workers rushed to his side and hovered around him helplessly, the soaked filter still filled with grounds released itself from the ceiling where it was momentarily stuck and fell on the bunch of them, leading to a chorus of expletives both male and female as it sprayed their white shirts with the still steaming recrement. In the middle of his coworkers’ mad scramble to get free from what must have seemed to them a sudden hot and grainy cloudburst, Larry Dooney glanced at the line of customers who stood in open-mouthed consternation. He raised his hand to his face and whimpered “Oo-oo-oo” as he watched the blister advance like a wave past his wrist and up his arm. Perversely he lowered his nose to it and inhaled the smell of burnt skin.

He wished he could tell the dentist about that episode and its aftermath, the trip to the emergency room, the ointment, the dressing, and the antibiotics, the entire treatment eventually coming to naught during the overnight romp in the Lake Michigan sand dunes. There, further medicated with the cool soothingness of Colt 45 ale he played until nearly daylight and later woke in searing misery, the wrapping gone from his wound and what little ointment remained infiltrated with grains of sand. But, of course, with his mouth wide open and the dental tool atomizing one of his upper incisors he couldn't say a thing and, besides, he figured that the dentist wouldn't appreciate the tale anyway.

There are all kinds of things I'd like to tell people, he thought now as he walked down the street, away from the bottom layer of hell which the good Lord had just given him a taste of and toward the distant plant where he would apply for a job that he knew would prove to be just a thin layer higher. But some things you just can't tell people. What should I say? he thought rhetorically about his request for a job application. That I just came here from a concentration camp experience and I deserve to have a job on the assembly line for the summer? That you won't even have to insure me because if I lose a few fingers, or even my whole hand in a punch press, I won't make a sound? That I'll just wrap the son of a bitchn stump up and go back to work and stitch it up myself before supper? He stopped, held both sides of his head again, studied the anthill that his new loafer had almost obliterated. Yeah, they'll hire me for sure, he resumed. "Yeah, kid," the worldly old personnel manager would snarl, "sure, come on board. We'll let you sit in the mezzanine and watch all the old veterans of the Big War, the shot at and the maimed and the impromptu medics working with hands that stuffed intestines into their buddies' gaping bellies, and when you think you're ready to stick somebody's eyeball back into his socket we'll maybe give you a broom to push. Either that, or you can get the hell out of here and grow up a little bit and be ready to feed a family instead of candyassing around here for two months before running off to Fairyland University." Sure, he thought. Well, I'm not going to walk. I'm going to catch a bus. I think I deserve that.

He turned around, saw no bus approaching. Good, he thought. I won't have to hurry. Looking ahead, he recognized a stooped skinny figure standing at the bus stop a long block away. It was a man he'd seen at various places around town, always walking, appearing purposeful and in a hurry. In no hurry himself and with his head raging against the calamity it had so recently experienced, Larry Dooney found himself sitting on a step of a concrete stairway leading up a bank and to a two story frame house with a screened in front porch, one of a series of similar 1920s-era Sear and Roebuck Catalogue-ordered structures lining the avenue. Holding his hands prayerlike over his mouth and nose, as if protecting his lower face from an icy wind, he stared hard at an expansion crack in the sidewalk and fought to withhold tears. His brain formed no words, no words were sufficient to express what he had just endured, only a roaring sound in his mind, an inferno in a bottomless cavern. He wanted to cry and cry and cry, he wanted to shriek like a banshee in the night, like a mother bereft of her family, like an angry suicide in his final plunge down a rocky canyon. But he couldn't do it. Young men don't cry. Well, maybe during migraines. During migraines any exertion, however involuntary, is permissible. Any exertion, any display, no matter how pathetic, at least lets you know you're still alive. But other than that, young men don't show their terror, their agony. The tears sliding down the sides of his face in the dentist's office were the inevitable results of eyes tightly squeezed shut, that was all. An embarrassment. Tears without sobs or sound. With his mouth wide open he couldn't grit his teeth, after all. Clench his jaws. He had to do something as the dentist's hand forced the needle up into the gum behind the stub where his black tooth had for years mocked his adolescent good looks, and besides holding the chair's arms in a death grip squeezing the eyes shut behind those thick glasses seemed to be his only recourse. So those lachrymal drops didn't count as tears because he wasn't crying. Now he wanted with all his soul to rend the tranquil summer air with screams and sharp tears, but he wouldn't.

Though the burning odor of his rasped front teeth had irritated him, he had felt proud, even a bit smug, over the painlessness of the initial procedure. There were the constant vibrations and the occasional surprising tickles that shot through his head, and a feeling of invasion that his body sensed with the kind of tight alertness that it exhibits when a sudden loud noise rattles the building you're standing in. Occasionally something resembling an electrical current would zap him when a nerve was momentarily violated. But it was all right, he had gotten through it fine, and he smirked when recalling all his friends' horror stories about dental work. "It hurts like hell," they said. "Make sure they give you something to kill the pain." "Like what?" he asked. "Novocaine it's called. Make sure they give you novocaine. You won't feel anything with it." "Laughing gas," said one friend. "It's really weird." Anything. Make sure they give you something, anything: that was the universal warning. He had got nothing, and he flew through the first procedure with the ease of a Frisbee through air.

He got nothing for the second procedure either.

"You're not going to give me anything?" he asked, his eyes, big as goggles, magnified comically by the thick prescriptive lenses, lurching between the dentist's indifferent face and the implement his fingers, pinky slightly raised, held like a host in front of him. The implement looked like the kind of needle you use to inflate a football or basketball, only its point was sharp enough to pop either one. And it glistened. He noted that: it glistened. As it would in a comic book drawing, little lines shooting out from the tip. "Nothing?"

Dr. Wehrman smiled benignly. "I'm afraid we can't give you anything, Larry," he said. "We've got to get the nerve out, and in order to do that we've got to know when we hit the nerve. And we've got to know that we've got it all. If your mouth is numb, we wouldn't know when we hit the nerve. Now it's going to hurt, no doubt about it. But it'll be over before you know it and believe me it'll be gone completely and you'll never have trouble with it again."

In a state of impending hysteria, Larry wanted to tell him that he'd never had trouble with the nerve at all, that it never hurt at all, never. But he knew that no objection or qualification or correction that he were to make would do any good, and all he wanted to do was show his astonishment and fear, in the hope that the dentist would reconsider and give him a shot of novocaine or a whiff of laughing gas or something. Anything. Because if the dentist said it was going to hurt, then it was probably going to kill him. And he didn't want to die yet. He was too young. He'd just left high school, had graduated after all, had even been popular in spite of his horror of a mouth. He even had a framed photo of himself and his girlfriend, attired formally for the senior prom, both of them grinning like newlyweds, his lurid teeth prominently displayed. And he wanted to show her his new crowns, her, Janie, she of the beautiful teeth, she of the kindness, the graciousness to overlook his oral deformity, the beneficence. Dear Janie.

But wait, he thought. It's for Janie that I'm doing this. It's for her. Hell, I can live with these ugly fucking teeth, I've done it for years already, it ain't no big thing to me. But Janie. It's for her. And for me too, because I want to be with her. I really want to be with her. And I want to look good for her. Fuck a little pain. I can take a little pain.

"I wish I could drive you home, Larry."

"That's all right. Don't worry. I'll be okay once I get on the bus."

The would-be driver, who with his broad shoulders and lean torso looked like a snow shovel standing on end, leaned down and wrapped an arm around Larry Dooney's chest and helped him stand. "Oh Jesus," whimpered Larry.

"You gonna make it?" asked his friend Vince. "Give us a hand, Wally," he said to a third young man. Wally reached around Larry's shoulders awkwardly and gripped him tightly. Together they slowly climbed the stairs leading to the back door of the gym and exited into the empty playground. They had two blocks to traverse to the bus stop, where Larry Dooney was to catch the 9:20 bus to his neighborhood.

"I'll make it." He grimaced and took in a deep breath through clenched teeth as he struggled along. "Jesus Christ."

"You ran good tonight," said Vince. "You won it for us, man."

"Thanks, man."

"I don't know how you do it, you dumb shit. What do you do it for?"

"I don't know."

"Why didn't you ask Coach to drive you home?" asked Wally.

"I don't know. I hate to ask."

"What is it, the shin splints?" asked Vince. "Or the quads?"

"It's fucking both," Larry said. The shin splints felt like shattered glass, the quadriceps like meat chopped open with a cleaver. With the pressure of each step the shards of his ligaments cut deeper into his bones, and when he straightened his leg the cleaver thwacked his thigh with renewed force. "I wish the fucking things would fucking break off," he said

"Oh man," said Wally. "That can't happen. We need you in the City Meet."

"Don't come to practice tomorrow," Vince said. "Stay away. Sit in the whirlpool."

At the bus stop he stood helpless as a post, supported by his friends, their voices mere hollow sounds in the night, whooshes of traffic blowing by, an occasional siren intruding on his solitariness. When the bus came his friends helped him up the two narrow steps and dropped the fare into the glass receptacle and helped him sit down. "Don't come to school tomorrow, man," said Vince. "Stay home."

"I can't."

"See you then."

It's so good to not have the stench of Ben-Gay following you around everywhere, he thought, and to not have to walk around all wrapped up in Ace bandages all the time. He inhaled deeply and felt himself relax. I hurt during track season about all that I could be hurt, he thought. This needle can't be any worse. So he's going to take out the goddamn nerve. It can't be any worse than getting scraped by a sharp twig.

"It's good to see you relaxing," Dr. Wehrmann said. "That'll make it a lot easier."

"It'll be over in no time," the assistant added.

"And it won't be long before you'll forget the feeling altogether."

"That's good," Larry said. "Cause I've got to go over to GM after this and apply for a summer job."

"You'll be able to do that," smiled Dr. Wehrmann. "And you'll be able to talk a lot better than if you still have novocaine in your jaw. That might deaden the feeling, but it numbs your mouth and makes you talk funny. Are you ready?"

"All set."

He wasn't set for long. He opened his mouth and watched the dentist's hand descend out of sight with the needle between his fingers and then he felt the initial prick lead into a searing shock of pain that shot helter skelter through his head like an unending lightning bolt. Every muscle, every tissue in his body tightened as one, contracted, like a suddenly soaked hawser. He was aware of his hands squeezing the heavy plastic of the chair arms, of his eyes widening and crossing and rolling upward and around, of a sound squeezing through the narrowed passageway of his constricted throat. And then the dentist's hand appeared with the needle and his began to relax, to sag even. He tasted blood. The assistant gently touched his gum behind the tooth with a soft square of gauze as the dentist uttered something vaguely congratulatory.

"Did you get it?" Larry asked.

Dr. Wehrmann looked surprised. "Oh no, not yet," he said. "We've just begun. There's a long way to go yet. But you're a tough young man, I can tell. You handled the initial probe very bravely. But we do have a way to go just to get up to the nerve. A couple of more probes should do it. Are you ready?"

As Larry nodded the dentist positioned himself and Larry saw his hand swoop down and disappear again and his body tightened this time before the shock, before he felt the violent current shoot like a thread of supersonic quicksilver through his head, acicular, unimpeded by molecule or atom much less matter of any density, his entire being, no, all Being itself, now consumed in a flame of pain infinite and relentless. And then he saw both the dentist's and his freckled assistant's faces gazing at him, Dr. Wehrmann's brow creased and his eyes penetrating. Another minute and Larry Dooney's body loosened and he shook his head to clear it as he gradually regained his sense of reality. But his mind was blank, his consciousness flat as a sidewalk. And then, again, the doctor's hand swooping and disappearing...

"I like to paint," said the little man at the bus stop. "I'm real good at it too. I'm going over to a man's house now to look over his place before I start painting it. I've got to find out what colors he wants, and I'll have to see if he has any ladders. I just got finished painting a place yesterday. Took four days. He had all kinds of stepladders, and I used three different ones. One of them was aluminum and the other two were wood. I like the wood ones best but I had to try the aluminum one. It felt good to climb it and stand on it. But I didn't want to take a chance on spilling paint on it because it looked so shiny and new. So I really didn't use it. For a really good painting job you need to use the right equipment, and wooden ladders are the right equipment, not aluminum ladders."

The man was slender and slouched. He had a small face that looked like an archaeologist's find with a nose. The forehead sloped and the nose was long and pointed, and his face inclined a long way before the chin abruptly receded almost to his Adam's apple.

His face showed a childish excitement, as if he had just ridden on a rainbow. A thick gray scar coursed his scalp from his widow's peak down along his right temple to behind his ear.

Larry Dooney studied him, listened carefully, watched his eyes move slightly and then stop, as if he caught sight of something, a mite maybe, or maybe an orchid, then move again, then stop, like a driver in heavy traffic, move and then stop, move and stop. But his mouth never stopped, and his focus and direction were firm and sure. Where did this guy come from? Larry wondered. What planet did he fall from? He had started in as soon as Larry stopped at the corner. First he greeted him and then he began his recitation.

"You have to be very careful with the paint so you don't leave streaks," he said. "So you have to look every time you dip your brush, you have to look first at your brush so that you don't drip any paint on the wall or on the floor, and then you have to look at the wall where you painted to make sure there are no streaks. And if there are, you've got to try to smooth it down."

"You sure do," Larry acknowledged politely. "I can understand. It's really important."

"It sure is," the little man reaffirmed. There was no stopping him, Larry Dooney now knew. He would have to stand here and then ride the bus with him until who knew when. He would have to stay with this man and listen to his almost nonstop chatter and study his face, study those ridges and those fine lines extending from his nostrils to the corners of his mouth, and that infernal scar on his scalp that made Larry shudder with a flashback to the needle in his nerve. And he would have to study those gray eyes that were seeing things that he couldn't, that were revisiting things that he could only imagine. And then the voice halted as those eyes made contact with Larry Dooney's. They peered into his eyes for the length of three labored breaths, and he studied those gray eyes in return, and he felt a contact with some unnamable thing such as he had never before experienced, not even in the twilight with Janie. But before he could become self-conscious the gray eyes moved away and the voice resumed. "But mixing the colors, that's what I like best," the little man said as the bus's squealing brakes signaled its approach.

Through the thick moisture built up on his eyeballs, Larry Dooney could barely make out the distorted face of Dr. Wehrmann. Too weak to lift his hands to his face, he sagged on the chair as the assistant gently removed his glasses and wiped his eyes. When they were reasonably clear and the glasses returned, he saw the dentist gazing at him with the kindly patronage of a kindergarten teacher anxious to treat his pupil to a new tidbit of knowledge. He held the needle in front of Larry's face and said, "Would you like to see a piece of your nerve?" Larry's focus slowly shifted from Dr. Wehrmann's features to a tiny gray piece of matter pierced by the point of the needle. It looked like a food particle from between his teeth after a meal. He wanted to say, "So that's my nerve, huh?" but he was too spent to move his lips or to summon even a groan of appreciation from his larynx. Finally he managed a feeble nod, a signal to Dr. Wehrmann to continue. "This is the beginning," he said. "We'll only need to go in there a few more times to get the rest of it. Can you make it? You're doing fine. It'll be over before you know it."

The part of Larry Dooney's brain that dealt with language no longer seemed to function, so he was unable to respond to the dentist's friendly reassurance even with private sarcasm. He was a worm now, a thing with mass and wiring, a reactive thing that slumped inert until a barbed hook was inserted into it. Unlike a worm, though, he didn't curl up and writhe when he felt the hook. Rather, the fatless putty that constituted his helpless form would in a flash turn rigid as an oak plank, firm enough to support a half-track across a canyon. Without language his mind worked by imaging and feeling alone, much faster than with syntax and diction, so in the brief moment before the needle penetrated his wounded gum he thought of the headaches. The leg injuries were forgotten now, the torn muscles and frayed ligaments and burst blood vessels relegated to the memory vault that contained old jokes, bathroom humor, the myriad inanities of youth. Now he was into the serious stuff: the headaches. And then the needle hit the nerve again and his body stiffened like a poker and his hands gripped the chair arms as if trying to merge with the plastic. The hinges of his jaws crackled like a burnt transformer and tears oozed out of his squeezed shut eyes as the current of pain filled every filament of his being at lightspeed, and then he was left to sag again and the mind, still inarticulate, returned to the headaches.

Larry Dooney never knew what was worse, the constant thunderous bolts of a brain trying to break through his skull or the desolation of enduring such torture alone. If his mother or brother sympathetically heard his plaintive mewing, his uneven panting, his rasping moans, or saw him on the sofa or his bed lying on his doubled-up legs with his face deep in his pillow, they nevertheless had no idea what he was going through, he was quite alone in the universe, a universe of spinning nausea and cudgeling blows. "Did you take some aspirin?" his mother would ask. "Your Aunt Martha used to get these headaches too. She used to take a little whiskey and some honey. Would you like a small glass of whiskey? Maybe that'll help you sleep." As kind as her offer was, it bounced off him like a hollow reverberation, a wisp of breath emitted by a sparrow. For all he wished for during these cataclysmic episodes was obliteration, an erasure of his own being as well as of the entire cosmos, which during these solipsistic episodes were identical anyway.

Listless, he stares at his soggy corn flakes and gingerly bites his toast. Another migraine day home from school, another missed practice. Even if he felt normal later, he wouldn't be able to practice with the team after missing school. I thought that one was going to kill me, he thinks. I thought it was all over. Sipping orange juice, munching the toast like a toothless old man, his stomach still feeling violated by the ceaseless day and a half long neurological surge through his system, he wonders, at the age of sixteen, about the value of longevity. He shakes his head, gently, gently, in delicate negation, gently, gently, lest his sadistic brain recall its grim prankishness and start the drum banging again. Gently. Then he stops. His eyelids widen almost imperceptibly then relax, the only movement he allows on his face, skittish yet as he is, scared that even a twitch of facial muscle might trigger a relapse. He sees something—something he can't describe, something with no features or dimensions, something that's everything and nothing, and he's struck by its beauty, its emptiness, its safeness, its absolute desirability. Muscles around his mouth and eyes move, reshape his face, ever so slightly, he's lost, reverie consumes him, the allure of nonexistence, the elegance of nonbeing. He sits transfixed, beatified, his toast slips out of his fingers.

Seconds—minutes?—pass. The vision ends, self consciousness returns, though he remains stationary, impassive. If, he reasons, being equals pain and its opposite, obliteration—beautiful obliteration, yearned for during headaches like air by emphysemics—if obliteration is the only relief, then why would I ever want to Be forever? Why would I ever want any kind of afterlife? And why would I ever want anybody or anything to wish that for me? Or plan it? Why would I ever want to even think that anyone would ever inflict such a thing on me? Or on anyone? You'd have to be a masochist to want to Be forever. And you'd have to be a sadist, a sadist of cosmic proportions, to want to inflict immortality on anyone. In full smile now, beaming as if feeling Janie's sweet fingers on his neck, he is suddenly light, airy, like a lingering thought, and he knows something is changing in his life, a shedding of weight, a molting of dross, a delicious sinking into a froth of solace.

"My favorite part of painting is cutting," said the little man with the wandering eyes. They sat together on a nearly empty bus reeking of diesel fumes heading crosstown. "That's the most fun."

"Why's that?" asked Larry. "I always thought it was the most tedious."

"Yeah. Well I like it. Because I'm really good at it. I like the way the paint goes on the wall up at the ceiling and is a different color from the ceiling. I like to make the straight streak up there with a different color of paint. I'm really good at that. I'm real steady too. When I was young I wanted to paint pictures on walls. My hand is very steady, and it's got to be steady when you don't use any tape or anything."

"You don't use any tape? It must take you a long time to do the cutting."

"Yeah. I can cut really fast because I'm real steady. I used to draw really nice lines on walls with a fine brush and then fill them in with paint. Lots of colors. Now I paint the whole walls, not just pictures. But the cutting up by the ceiling, that's what I like best. Because I'm up on the ladder, way up there, and I can get real close to the paint and that makes me very careful, besides my hand being steady…" Larry Dooney surveyed him as if memorizing details for a future contest. The man had specks of paint on his worn oxfords, his cotton shirt and trousers were gray like his eyes and were carefully creased and ironed. There were no wrinkles in the cotton, at least not from work, but small loose threads reached out from his button holes and from his frayed pants cuffs. The man was a marvel to him. His mouth moved with facility and with constancy, and never was a word lost or garbled, though occasionally he had to suck up some white spittle that seeped out. As the man talked about paint and cutting and ladders on this stinking bus, Larry had a sudden impulse to jump up and dance. He wanted the little man to dance with him too, he would lead and the man would follow and he would talk and talk and talk, and they would call the free new dance "The Paint" and the world would be free of pain, and they would whirl and flail their arms as if slapping enormous swatches of color on the air and they would leap like great open-mouthed frogs into space forever, the great vaulted stretch of unlimited liberation, he and the little guy with the scar as wide as the horizon.

The bus slowed as it approached a traffic light and Larry Dooney looked out the window and saw that they had entered an industrial area, and he saw the factory that was his destination. He looked at the man who had just begun a new dissertation on the mixing of paint when the vehicle stopped. "Shoot. I've got to get out," he said to the man. The man turned to him, he swiveled his head back and forth and said, "I do too." Larry pulled the buzzer string and they both got up and hurried to the opening door and stepped down and outside. "I really know how to mix colors real good. I've got a special eye for colors," the man said. "I know you do," said Larry. He wanted to say, And I want to hear all about it. I want to hear everything you have to say, and I'd like to walk all over town and not stop until you've run out of words. But he held back. The spell was broken. The bus pulled away in a black diesel cloud and the man stood still, as if waiting to be told to continue. "I've got to go," Larry told him. "I've got to go over to that factory over there."

The man turned around. "You work there?" he asked. "You paint?"

"No. I'm just going to go over there and apply for a job. If I get one, I don't know if it'll be painting or what."

"Oh," said the man. "Well, I've got to go to a friend's house to look it over so I can get ready to start painting. I'm going to start in the dining room."

"Okay. Do a good job now."

"Yeah. You know I will. I really know my painting." He looked around, seemed to choose a direction, and walked away, raising his hand as if offering a wave. His steps were short and he sort of tilted to the side of his lead foot as he jerked along. A few strands of blond hair stood up from the crown of his plastered head and danced in the breeze like wisps of thin wheat. "See you around town," shouted Larry Dooney, and the man's arm rose a bit and his wrist flicked in acknowledgment.

Larry turned to confront the sprawling brick automobile plant across the wide avenue, past the vast parking lot filled with gleaming cars, and he thought of crossing that expanse and asking someone for directions to the personnel office and climbing stairs to humble himself before a stranger in order to get a form to fill out for a job that he didn't want. Especially now, for some reason. He thought about what he really wanted. What he really wanted was to go home and call Janie and then to go to work for the rush hour at the fast food restaurant where he was happy earning a dollar-ten an hour and then have Janie pick him up so they could go to a movie. Where he would touch her and feel her warm breath in his ear. And afterwards in the park along the river he would feel her soft thighs beyond her stockings and her tongue in his mouth and he would swallow her juices, the two of them ensconced in the front seat of her car under the cottonwood sentinels.

He rode home on the next bus and grinned broadly at the window, inspecting in the reflection as well as he could the two caps that graced his mouth. They were small, and they didn't match the others in color, but they were only temporary. Maybe less than a couple of weeks. He had paid quite a price for them. By the end of the session with the dentist, all pride, all dignity, all sense of autonomy—all had wheezed out of his exhausted frame like air from a tire, and like a collapsed tire he lay splayed and shapeless on the hard chair as it was raised to an almost normal position. The caps were glued onto the stubs and the nerve was gone, pricked out centimeter by centimeter and wiped off on a piece of cloth like so much detritus from between dirty toes.

The reflected image of his face in the window glass gave way to the form of a little man walking almost mechanically, but purposefully, along the sidewalk. The man of the darting eyes, the man of the wandering scar. "I wonder what price he paid for that masterwork," Larry thought. The man faded from view and Larry settled down on the cushioned seat. He smiled. The pain was gone, only a memory. He felt contented. He had had the last word. In a sense. With Dr. Wehrmann.

"I'm just going to squirt some water in your mouth, Larry. It'll feel good. Just swish it around for a minute and spit it out. Open up now. It's only water this time." He held up a tube with a small nozzle on it, which Larry looked at languidly. He didn't trust it, and he didn't feel like making the effort to part his lips. "Only water, Larry. It'll make your mouth feel better." Larry separated his lips and his teeth and he felt a tube between them and then he felt a stream of cold water gather on his tongue and slide down and around it and toward his throat, which closed involuntarily and stopped the flow with only a feeble closed-mouth cough.

"Swish it, Larry. Just swish it around. And then spit it out."

In his dim state of consciousness Larry seemed confused by these directions, and he peered up at Dr. Wehrmann's concerned face. He saw Dr. Wehrmann nod in encouragement. Tentatively, he began to move his mouth, then he added a swerving of his jaw. He felt the water slosh in his cheeks, around his teeth, under his tongue. It was warm and tasteless, but it did indeed feel good. He was just beginning to delight in its lovely fluency, its refreshing vivacity, when he heard Dr. Wehrmann's voice resound as if in a cave, "You can spit it out now, Larry."

Taken back by this intrusion into his revival, Larry stopped swishing and raised his eyebrows as if told to drown himself. "Just spit it out now," the voice repeated.

Larry's eyes darted like a housefly. Spit it out. Where? Though his mouth and his spirit were alive again, his body remained inert. What does he mean? Where do I spit? He felt perplexed, not panicky, at his inability to respond to the doctor's command. What the hell?

"Just spit it out, Larry."

Indeed. With what force he could muster, his head cushioned on the chair back and his body still slumped sluglike, Larry took in his breath and spat a fountain of warm salivated water straight up like a geyser, right into the nearby features of the unsuspecting Dr. Wehrmann, who leaped away and in one fluid motion found a towel and wiped his face and flung the towel across the room. "In there." He motioned to the basin alongside the chair. "In there, damn it. You spit in the basin. You don't spit on your doctor."

Unable to talk yet, Larry did the only thing he could. He looked at Dr. Wehrmann and his face loosened and a smile broke out and grew until it reshaped his whole face and then he opened his mouth and he laughed. And he laughed and he laughed and he laughed, and the room resounded with a laughter that wouldn't fade and wouldn't fade and that later followed him outdoors and found him on this bus and that would fill him now and would shape his days and all his nights to come.

THE RACCOON'S SORE SNOOT

"Get out of here. Out of here. God damn it, get out of here you goddamn pest." Something much larger than the raccoon's head came down hard near her nose, something black and shiny with skinny floppy things flying around as the big thing went up and down, up and down, hitting the floor near her, making a racket louder than the other roar of sounds coming out of the mouth of the big guy clutching the black thing. The raccoon pulled her nose out of the small space and backed up a few paces, not too fast or too far because the big guy didn't seem inclined to emerge from his thin shelter to threaten or chase her. All he did was make those roaring noises and lie down again, the din fading to a mutter, when the raccoon backed off.

The raccoon stood there for several minutes assessing the situation. She ought to just leave, find some other source of nourishment, but the aromas coming from that space, inside that smooth skinned shelter, were so abundant and so inviting that she figured one more try would be worth it. There were salty things and yellow, almost rancid little blocks of things and, oh best of all, oh heavens alive, fresh smelling fish maybe just brought in and cleaned, mmm, maybe perch, yes, her favorite; and there was the spongy white stuff that she loved, even when she had to spit out the crinkly stuff that surrounded it. And the thing was, there were these spaces at the foot of the shelter that were so inviting to the raccoon, spaces that all the other shelters in this area didn't have, they were all sealed tight, but this one wasn't sealed all the way, only half of it was, the other half was only pinched at these intervals by some funny looking very thin things that shined in the needle of light coming from inside the shelter and by some bigger, strange looking things, much heavier but also shiny.

These bigger things had round heads and what appeared to be jaws clamped down and holding together the bottom and the see-through side of the shelter where the big guy entered and exited during the light hours just before the dark took over. These jaws wouldn't yield even when the raccoon swiped at the long, hard, stiff tail that was attached to the head. Usually that bottom and see-through sides were held together by tightly closed little teeth that ran along the whole bottom, but with this one the teeth only held together half of the see-through side and the bottom, and these weird heavier, clunkier things and little skinny shiny things held the other half together. They were clamped tight, but they left these spaces big enough for the raccoon to get her muzzle through, and she just knew that if she worked hard enough she'd be able to thrust her way through that space, maybe forcing some of those jaw things off, which would help a lot. In any case, she recalled a few occasions of expelling some fairly big things through this little hole in her bottom, and even though it hurt, it went to prove that difficulties like big things punching their way through little openings could happen with a little perseverance and a little time. Maybe with some quieter breathing, too.

She waited some time more and watched as the light dimmed within the shelter and finally disappeared. Except for some humming sounds coming from other shelters nearby and some distant "whip-poor-will" music, all was silent. She sniffed the aromas hanging in the still air—ah, that fish!—and followed her nose to the clunky things holding the bottom of the shelter to the see-through side. Using her multifaceted nose to feel an opening, she inserted it and carefully began to slide it forward until the firm barrier pressed against the bridge between her eyes. The idea of opening her mouth to see if the strength of her little jaws might make the thing yield a bit occurred to her, and when it worked she shot as much of her head through the expanded space as she could.

Unfortunately, she didn't get it in very far before the rim of the opening tightened around her head like some tough sinew, and she found herself trapped. She tilted her head back and forth as though boring though the impediment when suddenly a ray of light shone directly into her eyes and she heard the roaring of the big guy within. "God damn you, you little son of a bitch. Jesus Christ!" Blinded, she knew she was in trouble and she began a desperate attempt to retreat. She heard a loud "whomp" and felt a vibration and a rush of air, and she knew that the shiny black thing with the skinny floppy things had just missed her snout, she panicked, her legs and all her weight pulling hard, she finally got her snout out just as the black thing, quite hard and heavy, grazed the tip of her little black nose.

Throughout the friendly blackness into which she sped she heard the big guy's awful roaring. The cool evening air felt good on her nose. When she finally stopped, her heart still beating hard, she found herself safe on a low branch of a small scrub oak. She looked back toward the campground and might have thought,

"Well, that's that."

HER THINGS

High midafternoon clouds floated in from the west and south, met the moisture rising from Lake Michigan and swirled north and west and around, but slowly enough not to raise an alarm among the myriads afoot and in cars along the paths and roadway of the Outer Drive in October. All the thoughts that she'd entertained on the four mile walk along her beautiful Chicago streets, first along Grant Park and then up Michigan Avenue and through the near North Side along Lincoln Park, past the zoo and along the north lagoon, were gone. Her legs aching slightly and her breathing deep and smooth, she peered into the murky water. Her eyes were intense but her face relaxed, the tip of her index finger lightly touching her lips. She had the sinking feeling that her Things in the water, her beloved Things for which she had no name, would not be seen today. She had walked all this way to see her Things, but once again they would not be seen today.

She had walked all this way. She had changed directions and forsaken the Shedd's Aquarium and turned north and walked all this way. She'd forsaken the whales, the lovely beluga whales, her large gentle cousins with their benignant smiles, and walked these miles in the hope of seeing her Things, and now her soul seemed to sink with the sureness that today, like so many other days since her magical swim with them in this golden Chicago waterway, they would not be seen.

And she was so certain that it was this waterway, this lagoon of the thousand yachts, this haven for ducks and hungry Canada geese, that she had shared with her Things, her miraculous Things. She had searched the city's rivers, had followed the lowly Calumet and the treacherous Chicago and the mundane Des Plaines, had checked out as many of their tributaries as she could, but she always returned to the North Lagoon. It was here, she thought. It had to be here.

She squatted, peered down into the dark water, looking for them. Dark and murky, the lagoon in its present state would never yield so much as a glimpse of them, she knew, no matter how much effort she exerted in trying to penetrate it. But she knew, too, that if they were to enter the vicinity, even sliding along the sludgy bottom as they sometimes preferred to do, she'd see the amber transformation, the mysterious glow so beautiful among white hulls and green lawns, the things' way of beckoning to her, inviting her for a swim.

And oh, what a lovely swim. She remembered the last one as clearly as if it had been yesterday, though it had been years ago now. That time, that time of all times: she recalled how she watched them swim beneath where she stood as if the water her eyes pierced was the air around her, clear and fresh without boundaries save for the smooth bottom, she remembered clearly, the bottom, like a sky down below, the cerulean bottom, over which they passed like fleshy straws of many colors, flexible and undulating like long tubular clots, streaming by, at first as fast as small fish and then, as her astonishment melted away and her eyes fastened easily on them, more slowly, recognizably. Snakes? Eels? Giant slugs? Trophy gar pike? They could be any or all of these creatures, though some of them wore broad multi-colored bands and seemed interminably long. Through the still golden water, over the deep blue bottom, they surged innumerable, flowed, rushed; and then a strange thing happened. The world turned silent and she was among them, coursing forward like tranquil energy, a dart through space. She was there, in the water with them, moving more or less at their speed, though some could become dazzlingly fast as if showing off to her, moving smoothly with her arms at her sides and her feet together as though shot from a cannon. She wasn't a bit startled, but she felt enveloped by wonder, and she felt amused, and she felt at ease, at home with these things, these creatures, these straight, firm, unflappable pilgrims to some farflung destination. And she felt the cool of the water though, strangely, not the wetness. She looked straight ahead and to her sides at the graceful club shaped things, so she could not see but she could feel her clothing, she was still dressed, but her skirt and sleeveless knit top didn't seem to have any weight. She wagged her pointed feet and felt no shoes, but she had no concern as to their whereabouts. As her head tilted slightly to her left she saw a thing seem to materialize next to her. Much longer than she and about her thickness, it wore a textured skin of broad black and yellow bands, its blunt front end and its tail black. It slowed, passed, then without losing its rigid shape stopped and awaited her. As she drew alongside it, its head turned a bit and its eyes, black in black but rimmed with silver, gazed on her, and its tiny slit of a mouth seemed to smile.

Suddenly all was black and she didn't even know if she was moving anymore, even when she saw a distant glow become larger, larger, amazingly large, and then burst open like a fan into planes of bright colors, mainly yellow and yellowish ocher, diamond-like in the center and becoming circular as it expanded, a Picassoesque riot of sensation that engulfed her wildly and absolutely and then just as abruptly disgorged her into a placidity so spacious and profound that she thought she was dead. She was still underwater but all seemed clear bright space and she was barely moving now, delighting in the multitudinous cavorting things. Her long banded guide joined by two duplicates, they curled and undulated like playful neophytes newly introduced to the pleasures of aquatic coolness. Behind them other forms took shape, clear and gleaming, the shapes of walls and archways, lovely castle-like structures of limestone and crystal blinding in the soft, still, golden water.

And there it ended. With a sharp intake of breath she had lost consciousness and memory, and she later found herself lying in the late afternoon sun on the expansive lawn along the Lake Michigan shoreline. After waking she looked around and broke into tears, sitting there in the dried brown grass of mid-July, and joggers who took a break to check on her said in wonderment as they knelt beside her, "Easy, my dear. You're crying so hard you've soaked your clothes."

"Hey! You all right?" It was the second or third time she heard the bass male voice, but this time it penetrated her consciousness, and, startled, she raised her head. She was crouched close to the ground like a cat prepared to pounce, her head and shoulders extended over the water beyond the edge of the concrete promenade. She saw a heavyset old man seated on a portable camp chair about thirty yards away, fishing. He called again, "You okay?" Embarrassed, perplexed, she rose awkwardly and brushed off the knees of her slacks. Brushing hair back from her face, she smiled like a child caught in some forbidden act and called out "Yes. Yes" with a forced playfulness. "Of course." She walked in his direction. "I…I just was looking for my earring," she said. "My earring fell into the water." The man nodded and resumed the study of the bobber on his fishing line.

He was perched at the north end of the lagoon, on the edge of a concrete walkway beyond which, on a strip of grass between it and a shaded playground, was a solitary bench, and she hurried to sit down. She sighed. What she beheld was a postcard scene: the man's broad back covered by a dark gray vest, the dark lagoon filled along the west side with dock after dock of moored cruisers not yet taken out for the winter, the green lawns of Lincoln Park stretching far to the south where the scene merged with the northern face of the downtown area, starting place of the Magnificent Mile, the old Drake Hotel, Bloomingdales and the Hancock Center and all the wonderful architecture that she couldn't get enough of, and there it all was, greens and grays, stone and steel, all those straight lines and right angles towering above the lush crowns of the park and the Gold Coast, all that beauty, and she sat there, knotted up like a worn and dying pine tree, her neck tense and her teeth gritted, her fists clenched.

Damn! she thought. Damn damn damn damn damn! Shit! They don't know. They just don't know. And damn it, they just wouldn't believe it!

That's the trouble. You go around carrying this extraordinary, this amazing experience inside you and you want to share it and you can't. You can't! Nobody would believe you. They just wouldn't. They just can't understand. Damn it. They can't...Because it's true. It's true, damn it. It's so true. She knows it's true. She knows. And she can't tell anybody. Anybody at all. No one.

With that she relaxed, she felt her body softening, that good feeling, that retreat, that sad slide into the comfort of solipsism. It was that simple: She could tell no one, no one would ever know, just like other things that she kept private, locked up somewhere deep in the sacred grottoes of her soul. Billy.

Billy. She closed her eyes, blocking out the city. Billy. Billy. His name rained on her languid spirit like falling stars, a shower of Leonids in a vast hollow space. Her lovely Billy. Killed in a hunting accident at seventeen. Ten years ago. Shot in the face with buckshot. Father, with that fucking leer of his: "Well, looks like we won't have to look at his pretty face around here anymore. You can take that picture down now." Mother, indifferent, distant. Never said a word. "Rey! Rey! He's dead, he's dead. Rey, he's dead." Brother Rey. Her brother. Sneered. Walked away.

Grimacing, she opened her small pouchlike purse and extracted a half pint flask of vodka, looked around casually, and stared at the fisherman's broad back as she unscrewed the top and filled her mouth. She swished the smooth liquid around her mouth while returning the flask to her purse, then downed it in three swallows, made the usual involuntary face and shook her head, then waited for the first hint of its effect, her gaze expanding to drink in the downtown skyline and the scudding clouds across the October heavens.

• • • •

"You mind if I share your bench?"

Teresa tilted her head, eyed the young man, younger than she by a few years, nice looking, and nodded. What am I going to put up with now? she thought.

He settled down at the other end of the bench, snorted lightly, crossed his legs. He wore stylish basketball shoes and a red trimmed white warm up suit with the Bulls logo on the thigh of the pants. "Been here for a while?" he asked.

"A little while."

"That guy catch any fish since you've been here?"

"Not that I've seen."

"He never does that I seen," the young man reported with a forced laugh. "Nothing respectable anyway. Once in a while he catches a little perch about like this"—he held his fingers about three inches apart and Teresa looked and smiled—"that's all covered with little black spots. Usually they swallow the hook and he pulls it out and throws them back in. The gulls love him."

When's he gonna hit on me? Teresa thought. Jesus, I don't want anybody hitting on me now. Not now. Tonight maybe. Day off tomorrow. But not this guy.

"I don't know what he'd do with anything he caught here anyway," the man continued. "Can't eat that shit from the lagoon."

"Maybe he likes the view. Maybe he just likes to sit there and enjoy the view. I do."

"Yeah, the view's nice. My name's Tony," he said. "Antonio. Tony."

Teresa more than glanced at him for the first time. Nice looking, she thought. Bahamian? Bronze skin, gorgeous thick black hair tightly curled, smooth forehead over full black brows. A cleft in the chin. Nice. She smiled. "Hi."

"Yeah, it's really nice around here. I like to ride my bike to the zoo, then park it and walk around. Sometimes I stay around there, sometimes just walk. Today's a walking around day."

Teresa raised her eyes to the clouds racing along against the deep blue background, her head moving like a tennis spectator's, wondering what he wanted. A piece of her ass? Just her phone number? Maybe her purse. She looked over at him and saw nothing that gave away his intentions. Her eyes dropped to her purse not quite a foot away from her hip on the seat. Smiling, she decided to play the game. The cliché. Girl meets boy on a park bench. They begin cutely to engage in chit chat. "Yeah," she said. "I've done some walking today myself. From Grant Park all the way here."

"Grant Park?" He raised his eyebrows. "Girl, that's a long way. You walk that far all the time?"

"On good walking around days I do. I only worked a half day today. I was going to go to the Aquarium, but then decided to come up here."

"You live right around here?"

"Not right around here. But not too far away. But I like to come here. I like to just come here and sit and think and listen to the traffic, and I like the view. And sometimes I run into friends here."

"Well, here I am," he said with a wide grin. They both laughed and Teresa thought, "Oh God."

"So," he continued, "what's on your mind?"

"What do you mean?"

"I mean, what are you thinking about today while you're listening to the traffic and enjoying the view and meeting a friend?"

For a moment she was silent, wishing she was having some fun at this play, but Billy reentered her mind. Billy. He was doing that regularly lately, popping up unannounced, like a dandelion, pretty and bitter. It was getting to be a bit frightening. And her father, too, his leering eyes, his churlish farmer's hands. Billy never spoke, but her father's voice reverberated in her head, things she didn't want to think about now. It's so silly and so stupid, she thought. It's just so morbidly stupid. The game with this slick looking enigmatic young guy was, if not fun, at least preferable for now. At this time. In this specific place.

"Why do you want to know what I'm thinking about?" she asked him with feigned pleasure and a smile. "What are you, a student shrink or something? Looking for a case study?"

Her friendly tone encouraged him. He swiveled to face her, resting an arm on the back of the bench. She couldn't see his eyes through the dark glasses, but neither could he see hers. "Nope, I'm not a student shrink. But I am a student. I'm an acting student at DePaul. Second year. So I'm interested in people. What's going on with them. Inside them. You know?"

"Oh yes." She smiled exuberantly, tilted her head back. "Yeah, inside. Well, I can tell you that I've got a bunch of gas giving me trouble right now from a couple of hot dogs I bought over on Clark. God." She held her hands on her waist and looked troubled. "And I can tell you that it…"

"No no no," he said, and they both broke out in laughter. "No, not that." He looked down at where she held her hands and she noticed his eyes fastening for an instant on her purse.

"What then?"

"You know." He embraced his jaw with his thumb and index finger and slowly traced the line down to his chin. "Like, what's inside a person. The mind, you know? I'm a student of the mind. Of motivations, you know? The human spirit?"

She watched his fingers gently massaging his chin, now and then tracing the line of his lips. "Really," she said. "So, what kinds of parts have you been playing at DePaul? I'll bet leading man roles."

He laughed. Naïve child, he might have thought. "Well, I suppose you could say that. But not like Richard Gere types of roles or anything like that. More like Hamlet. And MacBeth. I like the meatier roles, you know what I mean? You know MacBeth?"

Looking impressed, Teresa pursed her lips and mouthed a "Wow." "That's really cool," she said. "I remember that play from high school. We studied it, and I actually read it, but I didn't understand it at all." What she did understand was that a sophomore acting student from DePaul wouldn't play MacBeth. Or Hamlet. He'd be playing an extra at most, an anonymous townsman or soldier. If he got a part at all. She had had friends from DePaul, and from Northwestern, and she knew a little about their reputations. So now she was satisfied: He was playing a con. Playing a fucking con. Jesus. All she wanted was a little peace, a little time to maybe see her Things, at least to revisit them, enjoy the October sunshine, waste her afternoon off. No bullshit, no come ons. Okay, she thought, what do I do?

Her mind worked quickly as she smiled in feigned admiration. What would the old man do? Daddy. What would Daddy do? Fucking Daddy…Don't go there, she admonished herself. Don't go there. She went there anyway. He'd probably bugger him, God damn him, she thought. Like he'd bugger most anything. That son of a bitch. She felt her smile fading, her eyes losing focus, lowering, imperceptibly she hoped, she knew she was drifting. That's all right, Tessie, she told herself. You can drift. That's all right. Rey? What would he do? Rey. Easy. He'd pull a knife on him right here. Slash him. Right here. Right in the daylight. With that fat guy fishing over there…Billy? Billy? No, don't do it. Don't do it. Don't… Jesus? What would Jesus do? She felt a smirk form, but inwardly she hissed. She inhaled sharply. Shit, she said.

She forced herself to raise her eyes, refocus, readmit him into her universe, him, her handsome adversary, her slick antagonist newly defined, in the moment or two that she had wandered lost in her own personal forest tangled of milkweed and poison sumac, nettle and thorny wild raspberry, by newly laid shadows crisp along his jawline, his strong handsome nose with its flared nostrils, the hollow under his straight left eyebrow. She looked at his hand, dangling carelessly off the back of the bench, the smooth skin, the graceful fingers with subtle knuckles, nice nails, not manicured but nice. Too bad he's not honest, she thought. I'd bed him in a minute.

"That's all right," he said suddenly. "We all get lost in our thoughts occasionally, don't we?" Assuming a new direction, she nodded coyly. "See?" he said. "I told you I'm a student of mind. Motivations. See? I knew."

"You got me there," she said after a reasonably convincing laugh. "Well, I guess there has been something on my mind, you know the usual, a work thing. Something happened at work." Yes, she thought, I'm going to spill it. Big deal. It won't do any harm, it's nothing that he'll learn about me. I can lead him on, make him work If he wants my purse, he'll have to work for it. It's all set for him, but he'll have to work.

"What kind of work do you do?" he asked, playing the naïve student to the hilt, his face alight with enthusiastic curiosity, the facial shadows alive with movement. "Wait, wait…let me guess. You're a, a—a model. A model. For a department store. One of the big ones." He continued animatedly in spite of her screwed up features, her look of derision. "Fields. No. Um, Bloomingdales? No? Okay, I give up. Where do you model? Lord and Taylor?"

"You've got to be kidding me," she laughed. "I'm five feet three. In my shoes. I'm no freaking model. Not even for kid's inflatable swimming pools."

"But you'd make a nice looking kid in a kid's swimming pool."

Teresa felt a disgust creep in now, its tentacles spreading like a headache. He's a shit, she thought. He's a stupid shit. He don't care how I look. He don't care shit about me. He wants my freaking purse and he'll say anything. He's like hair grease.

She nevertheless determined to play the game out. She could still look at him, she could still play the game, play coy, play mock assertive, play genuinely interested, play victim, and she could look him in the eye and smile, she had done such things numerous times, she had looked at her father and said "Daddy, Billy's dead," knowing full well what he would do, how he would look, the leer, the curled lip, the snort, not necessarily what he would say—"Well, looks like we won't have to look at his pretty face around here any more"—but something approximate to it, and she could look straight at him afterward and cry "But Daddy, Daddy, don't you know what this means to me? Don't you know what this means to me? Don't you know that I love him Daddy? Daddy?" And she could still look at him through the narrow watery cavities of her eyes protected now after his blow by her hands as one of them began to swell and blacken, her fingers separated enough to enable her to run toward his back as he turned and spat out "Bitch" at her and raised his hand to strike again. And turning she could look at the swimming shape of her brother Rey and plead "Rey? Rey? He's dead. He's dead," prescient too of his sneer and rejection. If she could follow through despite her loathing of them both, then she could play this scene out too, she could act this out too. So she assumed a pout and stuck out her chest. Under her loose blouse and partially buttoned flowing jacket her breasts wouldn't jut, but they'd be noticeable.

"Are you saying I look like a child?" she asked in a mock whimper.

"Oh my God no," he laughed. "I certainly didn't mean that. No, you look much more the woman than the child." Oh my God, Teresa mimicked to herself. He's awful. I bet he slaps his women when he fucks them. But despite her growing contempt, she complied with the rules of the game by softening her features and flashing a satisfied smile. Pleased, Antonio shifted on his seat. "But tell me, what do you do?"

"I'm a saleswoman," she said. "A clerk, in women's apparel. At Carson's."

"Ah, no wonder you dress so fashionably. You're right in the midst of fashion. Carson's. How about that. That's my mother's favorite store."

She'd worked there for eight years, she told him, dropping out of Columbia College because she liked the store so much better. Liked the feel of the place, the customers, even her bosses. Liked to be around clothes, enjoyed the colors, textures, felt good helping people in their selections. Loved downtown, the crowds, the noise, just like now, listening to the traffic on the Outer Drive, she liked that too, could go to sleep to the sound, the constant rush. Downtown she liked the car horns, the bus engines, the smell of their diesel fumes, the rattle of the Els, liked to stand under the tracks on Dearborn and feel the vibration. She gave change to the panhandlers and bought the Street Smart paper and ate lunch at the Greek restaurants mostly, she preferred the Greek flavors, the looks of the Greek men though there were as many Latino servers as Greeks, the pace and the noise.

"So what's so heavy about work this morning that it's been on your mind?"

She heard this voice. It broke into her distracted rambling, and she felt a twinge of resentment. Lowering her eyes Teresa collected her composure and asked what he meant. "I mean, you said that something happened at work that you've been carrying around inside of you on this beautiful day. And I, student of human feelings that I am, am wondering about it."

"Oh," she said. *Should I go on or should I end this silly game right here. Get up and walk away and leave him my stinking purse and go home and eat and wait for Benny or make him work a little more for it? God, how morbid you are. Perverse. But he's right about my carrying this thing around with me. This old lady. Maybe I should just talk about it and let it melt away so I can be happy for Benny tonight.* "Yes. That's right. Mr. Drama Student," she said, a bit too aggressively maybe. "So I am carrying it around with me. So? You know?. ." She looked hard into his eyes. She wanted to hit him, smash his pretty face with the edge of her fist. Instead she sighed with force. "You're funny, you know?" She had collected herself and she felt proud, every bit the actor. "Sitting down with a girl on a park bench and wanting to hear her tell about what happened at work this morning. Most guys would have been hitting on me by now, and some would be hitting me because of what I say to them for their hitting on me. But you're different." She swiveled a bit and threw one leg over the other and rested her arm on the bench back in a mock mirror image of the young man, who leaped from the bench laughing, gestured grandly with outstretched arms and bowed.

"Hah! I am different, that's true," he said and sat back down. "But you are too." After the clownish flourish his manner settled to that of a serious interlocutor, a detective or an academic. "One of the ways I'm different is I can tell that you're too smart to be hustled, and I don't like to play games I can't win. So all I want to do is talk and maybe learn a little bit and then be on my way. A harmless little interlude in the park on a lovely fall day, my highlight of the week. That's all I want."

Teresa smiled widely at him. She picked up her purse and, holding it close to her chest, pretended to rummage through it, though it was no bigger than a pillbox hat. "Ah," she exclaimed as she drew out the flask. "First a little nip." She closed the bag, unscrewed the cap, took a swallow and sighed. "Like a little?"

"Sure," he said, eagerly reaching for the plastic bottle. "What a surprise. You don't look the type to be carrying around a flask." He pulled a mouthful and swallowed it, a faint look of disgust flashing at her. After returning the bottle he wiped his hand hard on his pantleg. "Sticky," he said.

She shrugged and set the purse carelessly on the seat between their legs. "I don't know, there's not much to tell," she said. "It's just that this little old lady came in today and I had to help her pick out a black wardrobe. It was really weird, you know? This little old lady, probably in her eighties, so little. I can't get her out of my mind."

Antonio grinned indulgently. "So what's so memorable about an old lady who likes black clothes?"

"I don't know. This old lady was different..." *Face gray as a nightmare, eyes small and gray and moist, nose long and full but lips as thin as capillaries, body frail as a stumper mushroom, tiny, wispy, like a wraith, her appearance sullen, silent. "I want black." Her voice a squeak, demanding repeat. "Black," she says. "Everything. I'm starting all over with black."*

What do you say? "When one starts over, it's usually with pastels. Are you sure?"

"Black. Everything black. I'll never wear any other color. Show me your black. Pants, skirts, tops. Sweaters. Underwear."

"Oh, the underwear is on the third floor, Ma'am."

"Then I'll go to the third floor for the underwear. After I purchase the other things." The black things. She turns, her movements not painful but pained, she waits for guidance. The enormous space around them, blotched with displays, seems to darken, turn lugubrious, the canned music dims, the old lady already in black but with a plain snow white blouse, she sighs, Teresa's eyes roll upward: What have I got here? They're in a cave now, oppressive, joyless, a sudden descent into damp, mist, chill. "Where do we begin?" the old lady asks. Teresa had been preparing to leave for the day, a half hour until one, a walk to the Aquarium, the belugas all white and serene, their childish faces, smiles, they look right at her as they pass, so benign, they're so benign, they'd

bestow blessings on you if they had arms… "I suppose at the beginning," she says, aiming for a bit of levity. "I suppose with a size four." The guide, the light in the darkness, she leads the way to pants first, dressed in black herself today, black leading black to the black, a stream of black flowing between colorful racks and tables, the old lady keeps up with her stride, the pants are toward the front, there are windows there, some natural light. "Good that black is so fashionable. We've got lots of black in stock." Wool blends for the coming season. Lots of knits, knits are so comfortable, so carefree. "I don't care about comfort," the old lady says. "I don't care about carefree."

Slacks, sweaters, jackets, blouses, the shoes and hose are in another department, hats too, that's seven hundred and thirty-nine dollars. She signs a check with a shaking hand, Teresa initials it without question, her eyes tearing. "My daughter died," says the old lady. Sunken, lonely eyes, frightened eyes. Teresa studies those eyes and through those eyes she sees Billy, poor Billy, his name like a shower of stars, his face blown away by buckshot. She looks at the old woman with horror. So tiny, frail. "Unexpectedly. At home. She was only forty-eight. I'm eighty something and my daughter died alone at home. I'll wear black the rest of my life. Thank you for helping me."

Teresa felt a shudder assail her upper body, her shoulders and chest. "OD'd," she said, "or suicide." Poor thing. She leaned forward and stared stonily straight ahead, her hands clutching the edge of the seat, her arms rigid and shoulders hunched. Through clouded eyes she saw a mosaic of white trapezoidal shapes and their reflections in a still, dark surface and she saw a portly gray and white blob in the foreground and in the background roundish forms of ocher and red and yellow and other blotched fields of those colors rising from a distant green mat and she saw other forms, gray hard edged and geometrical, shooting up from those fields and her face took on a bemused, skeptical twist as if wondering what these images and shapes were doing there, what business they had being there without her prior approval. She tilted and lowered her head, looking past her left shoulder, and she did a subtle double-take at what she saw: It was a low arched bridge and a channel disappearing under it. Above was the pavement of the Outer Drive and on it whooshing by was the ceaseless traffic.

Her mind tuned out the traffic sounds and focused on the channel. She had been in that channel once, darting effortlessly in the dark with legs together and arms at her sides, and she emerged with her Things on the other side with the great yellow and black-ringed worm next to her, seeming to nod, and that was where she experienced the greatest happiness of her life. It was there, right there. Her face softened, her lips slowly formed a smile, beatific almost, she lifted her hands and gently cupped one inside the other, her body melted, she felt and luxuriated in each tiny segment of motion and time. As she sat back in the bench she looked down to her right to confirm the emptiness of the space next to her where her purse had sat, the emptiness at the end of the bench, and her smile stretched her mouth taut, her eyes glistened as though espying a desired Christmas present. And he took it! she exclaimed to herself, back in the world of things.

"Hah!" she said aloud. He did it. He did it. Hah! She had heard him too. She wasn't watching, but she felt his movements, she didn't miss much in this world, and she certainly didn't miss the thing she had most expected, even in the midst of her somewhat abstracted narrative of the old woman and the ensuing reverie she had drifted into. But she knew when he was reaching over for the purse, when he grasped it and stood up, when he tiptoed away from the bench and when he began to run. She even knew which way he ran, north, she heard his shoes on the parking lot pavement behind the bench and the strip of grass. Even sneakers aren't silent. Good job, Tessie, she thought. Tessie, the name Billy gave her.

She rose and stretched her arms out and took a deep breath. She felt around her clothing, felt her wallet in her right pants pocket, her lipstick and hand mirror in the left jacket pocket and a pair of scissors in the right one. Stretching her legs now, she caressed the muscles in her thighs and lower back, she twisted her upper body, and she prepared to leave. "Good bye, Senor," she called to the fisherman. "I hope you start having some good luck." The old man turned, nodded, and gave a cursory wave.

God I'm tired, she thought. What'll it be, walk bus or taxi? What the hell. Walk over to Sheridan and take the first bus or taxi that comes. I'll be home by five, shower, have a drink, wait for Benny. We'll have a nice meal tonight. She strode briskly, free of cares, past joggers and bikers and pet walkers, still smiling. Wait'll he finds out that part of him found his way to an actor. Hah! An actor!

She pictured the actor fumbling with the ornery little latch that always resisted her own nimble fingers, particularly when in a hurry. What would he do when it opened? Stick his hand in? Withdraw it in confoundment? Extract the nearly empty half pint bottle of vodka and raise it near his face, peer into the purse and catch the whiff of the effluvium of drowned rodent? Reach in and take out a handful of the contents and toss them into the air with outrage and disgust when he realized what they were: accompanying the dried mouse carcass five or six caked and sticky condoms, quite robustly expended, at least a couple of them, the supremely—what should one say—appointed ones, the thickly engorged and spiny ones, belonging to Benny? Oh, Benny will laugh when he hears of this. Either that, she thought, or he'll toss me out of the sack. A sudden thought struck her, oh how she wished she could have been in the sack with Billy, just once. Just once…She let the thought pass, no sense going there, no sense dealing with that baggage, and her mind returned fleetingly to Benny.

As she reached Cannon Drive to make her way to Diversey, she turned for a last glimpse of the lagoon, home of her Things, her beloved Things, who would be there again when she came, one of these times, they would be there to beckon her, and she would have no second thoughts, she would join them without hesitation, she would forsake Benny and all the rest of her lovers and even her beloved streets and the benign beluga whales at the Aquarium, she would leave them all. For under the swirling Chicago skies and within the plumes of the city's grandiose architecture and its pacific parks, she knows where her destiny lies, her special destiny, the end of her forlorn sojourn. And she is willing to abide patiently, to await the invitation which is sure to come, to hear the blips and bleeps of those long, twirling, tensile bodies, those unnameable Things, the Things of her calling.

THE RACCOON'S FINAL SWOON

Feeling she was finally safe, the raccoon shinnied down the oak trunk and found herself once again on the security of the forest floor. She had nursed her sore nose, grazed by a camper's black leather boot, and her biting eyes that had been lashed by the boot's whipping lace, for a good long time, and now the first small swarm of a new day's light appeared and she was plenty hungry. She was also confused. She should have a full belly by now, should be savoring a well deserved sleepiness, should be on her way to her lair to smack her lips as loud as she wanted and to lie down luxuriously for a nice undisturbed slumber. Instead, she was hungry and a bit dispirited. In this her favorite campground she had never been treated with such meanness before. Children merrily chasing her with squirt guns, leashed dogs lunging comically, some people sending halfhearted kicks in her direction—those were the kinds of threats she had to deal with, playful threats mostly, made by campers actually delighted with any wildlife they encountered, especially cute little guys like her and her kin, and of course, the black squirrels and the deer.

She looked toward the row of tents standing like craggy warts on the wooded slope and considered a last forage before sunrise, but recalling the hostility she encountered only a few hours earlier she elected to turn around and make her way back to her own shelter under some thick deadfall on a comforting sandy dune overlooking the great lake. Probably she'd find some nice tart wild grapes along the way, and she knew where lay the remains of a small bag of garbage she had hauled away and hidden a couple of nights ago for just such an emergency. Heh heh, she was one smart raccoon all right.

Lumbering quietly under the soft ferns on her skinny legs, she was making good time until her hearing was shattered by a sudden barking noise and a vicious snarl from behind and another series of barks in the other direction between her and her lair. Her heart stopped and then leaped into a furious pumping and she ran mindlessly to the safety of her lair where the dog, a large and barely distinct form, crouched surprised and delighted. As she swerved the dog grabbed her and she felt its teeth clamp down on her neck and she felt herself rise from the ground and fly briefly. She smacked something hard, a tree trunk, and bounced off and lay stunned for a moment before one of the dogs, she couldn't tell which, of course, lay claim again to her neck. But this time, alert now, she drew on every defensive resource she possessed, teeth and claws and speed of movement and her weight and her chilling caterwaul and she broke loose and lashed at her attacker until it yelped and withdrew. But not far. It stood and stared at her, panting, and suddenly there were two of them looking at her, assessing her. She returned their stare, her awl-sharp teeth bared, breathing hard too but ready for a fight. She knew she could take one of them without too much of a problem, but, because she had never before faced two such powerful adversaries, the second one frightened her. Probably she could make short work of the one, but two? On top of that concern, she now became aware of intense pain shooting through the back of her neck, into her shoulder and down one of her front legs.

She heard a snarl from one of the dogs. In the billowing dawn she could see it, a big hairy thing with sharp ears and short dark hair and eyes that seemed to burn red. That was the one she focused on. It snarled again and she bravely answered, her voice shrill and frightening and eerie. The dogs backed up a step or two and she repeated her raccoon epithet. But her bravado faded when she saw the big dark one dip into a nasty looking crouch and lower its ears. Its teeth glared and its distorted black gums quivered as it took its first slinking steps toward her. The other dog, black faced and mottled like a rotting log, moved to the side, its head turned toward her, preparing to attack from the flank. The raccoon snarled in a low tone this time, her voice raspy and deep and whiney, as if saying, "Hey guys, come on. That's enough, huh? Hey guys."

A tree stood a few feet away and she sprang for it and grabbed on and began desperately to climb but something sharp and heavy grabbed her hind leg just above the mid joint and pulled hard. Against a rush of pain she tried futilely to clamber up the slippery bark, she lost her grip and fell and as she hit the ground rolling and tumbling she felt the second dog's mouth on her throat, bringing her to a sudden stop and holding her down, the first still pulling on her leg. She tried to thrash but the weight of the dog on her neck held her like a burial stone and she felt her leg break like a stick and heard the crack at the same time, and the dog freed her now useless leg for a moment only before she felt its mouth around her haunch, the teeth digging in and pulling hard again, tearing her meat. That's when the second dog, sensing her relinquishment, released her throat in favor of her loin, sinking down into it and pulling with the ferocity and rage of a snaggled tempest. At this point all the pain she had felt coalesced into a numbing black cloud beshrouding her like a heavy blow frozen in time, she could no longer fight or resist at all, she could only thrash in the limited way her body allowed under the weight of the dogs. And she could shriek. Unfortunately no shriek from her gurgling throat could save her, none could call forth help, and in fact none could be heard above the greedy snarling of her ferocious killers. And then she felt things snap in her side and haunch like a heavy rubber band breaking as flesh separated from her flesh, and suddenly the heavy force was gone as the dogs retreated and the pain returned and filled her like a jolt of electricity that charred her entire being.

Mercifully, her pain was now so pervasive that, like Guido eternally consumed by his flame, her nervous system no longer differentiated it from nonpain, it was just there, like her fur, so she watched impassively the dogs' bloody mouths chomping rudely on her meat, saw the bone and torn flesh of her bedraggled leg and the pink of her intestine sagging in the dirt. She managed to turn her head and, summoning all her remaining strength, she forced her torn shoulder muscles to activate her front legs and pull her body forward a few inches. But with the movement came a nasty growl and she felt the force of another hammer blow on her shank, her body shook raggedly as the dog dragged her backward, its own head shaking as it worked to separate meat from meat. Then she fell, she let out another low raspy sound, it might have been "Oh, ooo, ow. Jeez, guys, that's enough, huh? Come on guys. Ooh, jeez it hurts. Oh jeez. That's enough now, okay?" But it wasn't. The other one leaped at her, had her by the throat, shook her like a hairy dimestore toy, his buddy joined in the game, and when they were done they spat out what was left and silently ran away.

EXERCISE

The Comfort Café stood facing east, awash with ten a.m. sunlight but nearly deserted. A few workers joined the owner in planning the late morning agenda, visited occasionally by a deliverer of breads or fresh produce. The music was called "adult," the voices from the kitchen were Caribbean, the décor was imitation French featuring oil paintings of village patisseries. A forty-ish woman, finished with her scone and latte, stood to slip on her leather jacket, picked up her package and newspaper, and strode across the floor to a late middle-aged man with a closed book on his table and a fluid face. His feet were under his chair and his hands lay folded on the table, and he seemed to be lost in an agreeable silent conversation.

"You look like you're enjoying your thoughts," she said.

He had looked up as she approached and he smiled during the slight pause before she spoke. He watched her mouth shape the words and then he jumped to her dark eyes and nodded with what appeared to be an old fashioned polite bow. "Well thank you," he said. "I am. Very much."

"It must be nice to entertain such thoughts on a workday. All I have are work thoughts and diet thoughts."

They laughed smartly. "Oh, but I'm very fortunate," he said. "I'm retired. My current work is to entertain such pleasant thoughts."

"Not a bad job. You'll make a lot of people awfully envious if they find out."

"I suppose that's true. Maybe we should just keep that news between ourselves."

She placed the paper under the arm that held her package and touched his shoulder with her newly freed hand. "Your secret's safe," she said. "But you'll have to promise that you'll remain diligent at your work."

"Absolutely. I promise you."

"So nice talking with you," she said. "I wish I could join you. But some of us must put in our obligatory forty hours."

"You must be on break then."

She sighed dramatically. "I just can't stay away from these scones in the morning."

He stood up and offered a little bow. "I'm sure I'll see you again in here. We could have a cup of chai."

"I'd love that," she said, starting toward the door. He watched as she pushed it open, turned the corner outside, and disappeared. He hadn't noticed if she wore a ring and he hadn't learned her name.

Picking up his cup, he ambled to the counter and asked for a refill. "Of course," answered the owner, a sturdy blonde woman with heavy lips and a husky voice. "That was the house blend, right? You don't want to try one of our specials?"

"Not today, thanks. The house blend is plenty good."

"Enjoy," she said. He smiled, nodded once and returned to his seat.

He sat down and crossed his legs, laying a forearm along his thigh and resting his other elbow on the chair arm. Unmoving, oblivious even to the coffee's fresh vapors, he thought of another time, another restaurant, another strange woman. Spaghetti on Chicago's north side, a second glass of wine, early afternoon. Lost in melancholy thought, Claire in the restroom, he had been startled by the judgmental voice of a woman who had risen from the next booth and walked past saying, "I hope you get treated for your disease." It seemed a voice out of the blue, no, out of dense gray clouds, without compassion or even a degree of warmth, and as he looked up she rounded a corner into an adjacent room, leaving him to consider this petty assault. She can't know how hooked I am, he had thought. How could she? It's only my second glass, and I'm eating and conducting myself smoothly, discreetly, as always. How could she possibly know? The problem was his and his alone. Nobody else knew about it, nobody. Not even Claire. Not his kids. Not his best friends. He turned to see the woman's retreating backside in the other room, her slim hips and long ponytail barely swaying. She must be guessing at something, or she's crazy, he thought, going around muttering at everyone she sees, remaining quiet for as long as she can tolerate being civil and then relieving herself by casting insults at harmless people minding their own business. He remembered her clearly now, her voice anyway, and her face too, though not so distinctly. He remembered how he had felt violated by her assault on his deeply protected secret, on the sanctity of his very soul. On his way out later he had passed her, sitting at another table near the exit, peering at him judgmentally through close set eyes along a long bony nose as he approached and nodded, smiling, at her.

That was some few years ago, maybe five, another lifetime. How could she have known, he wondered now. How could she have been so right? She must have been studying me really closely. She must have been there at some time herself, he thought, there, there, where he was at some time ago, some long time ago. So deeply in the throes. So deeply in the pain, the delicious and the terrifying mattress of addiction, sunk into its pliancy like a sad needy lover. Though he knew at the time that he was on a self-destructive path, he had no idea how far along he was. How nearly fatally along. The descent after that day had been precipitous and blindingly fast. So fast. And so nearly terminal.

Finally he moved, relaxed, sat back in his chair and sipped his coffee. He shook his head slightly as if in reverence. And now it's all changed, he thought. It's all so good. It's all so good. And it's going to get better. It's got to get better. It's got to. It already is getting better. It already is. Every day. All the time. Now if only Claire will come back. If only Claire. If only.

At home later, after the treadmill and the Cardioglide, after the sit ups and the blues by Taj Mahal, he approached his CD player and prepared to change the disc, his movements slow, methodical, utterly self conscious, but borderline entranced. What is this, he thought, if not pure self indulgence? He smiled. But that's all right. It keeps you humble. It keeps you in tune. He extracted a disc entitled *Appalachia Waltz* and inserted it and forwarded it to the second track, to the title track, then he retreated a couple of steps and separated his legs far apart. He waited a second before he heard the first note of Mark O'Connor's fiddle and then he slowly rolled his head back on his neck and extended his arms as if stretching to a new day, or to embrace a lover newly risen intact from a forlorn grave. Not satisfied that arm muscles were strained enough, he reached out farther, his fingers separated and tense, palms upward, and when he could no longer entertain the illusion that he could stretch them a millimeter more he began to slowly rotate his arms, slowly, slowly, until the palms were down, and then he continued the slow rotation, feeling the tension mount the entire length of his arms, the muscles taut and a mild pain trickling into the elbows, and then he felt the dopamine begin to kick in, feeling for all the world as if the sensation were in his arms and shoulders and not in his head, the beginning of that rich flush of electrochemical current associated with hardened and quivering muscles. Oh god, it's delicious, his mind whispered to him, but without words, without the mental sound that interferes with hearing, as the tenor voice of Yo Yo Ma's cello gently joined O'Connor's soprano, the high register of the violin met with the mellow voice in a lovely conversation in the hollows of some old eastern mountains. He bent and twisted his torso and slowly, gracefully swept his right arm through space and with his fingers together the flats of his nails touched the outside edge of his left foot and he slowly straightened and twisted the other way and touched his right foot with his left nails and inchmeal, achingly, he raised himself upright again, his head thrown back and his eyes closed as the two instruments made their elegant ways through the winding mountain passes, not meandering at all but carefully controlled, alive and in love.

Shaking his head slowly side to side, or circumscribing a tight oval, sometimes a figure eight, undulating like an exalted line in a Rembrandt engraving, his face as malleable as the dramatic low clouds whisking across the eastern sky over the stolid Adirondacks, sun descending, clouds with burred edges the colors of rose and peach and gold, and beyond them the calm blue expanse of the depthless sky, like the freely ranging tenor between the sweet guidance of the soprano violin and the steady bass foundation. Oh Claire, he thought, the words audible in his head, Claire, can you see me now? Can you see that I'm all right again? That I'm all right. The pain, the pain is gone, now, Claire, and I'm all right again. Can you see oh my Claire? The tears formed when he heard the alto for the first time, the voice of Claire, the husky voice, her sound of passion and of repose, the sound he missed with an unplumbable longing—the hole in his being—gone, like her arms, gone, like the brush of her hair against his face, her nipples drawing undulating patterns around his chin, his eager mouth. Gone.

A solitary drop slid from the pool in his eye down to the sideburn on his tilted head. He felt neither ashamed nor overindulgent in his emotion, for the tear whose path he could still feel, though rapidly drying. It's okay, he thought without words. I'm okay now. I'm more than any one thing, I've learned that. I'm alive. And life is so good. Life is so...good. So...manifold. So...so utterly harmonic. Like the flow of that tenor around the tors and the empty valleys of Appalachia, gliding, exploring, whole, guided by the heavenly soprano, supported by the firm and gentle bass, exhorted by the wraithlike alto.

As the piece ended he counted his seventieth repetition. Not finished, he returned the invisible ray of the CD player to the beginning of the track and when the violin commenced he reached as high as he could until his shoulder and arm muscles felt on the verge of tearing and he held them there, hands open wide and fingers taut and far apart, the dopamine that in other times, the good times with Claire, had seemed to seethe through his groin and legs with such delicious intensity now made his arms and shoulders and upper back burn with the same zesty intoxication. After a few moments he slowly bent down and touched the floor at the tip of his shoe and rose again, the chemicals unleashed in a torrent now, his face lit in a realm of ecstasy that intensified as the song progressed and the numbers of his stretches added up, leg and back and shoulder muscles taut as cello strings, flashes of sunlight blinding his closed eyes, memories of immersions in cold mountain pools, back in the flower days, the days of tongue and breath, of juices ambrosia rich, skin sweet as nectar…

…and oh God, oh God: in a flash the real-all-too-real imagery of suicide intruded, crashing through the sweet strains of his reverie: the blankness of his plunge down the dark and endless ravine ("The bad boy's going now," he told her, and to himself: "It's over. Finally." The words return over the violin, the sweet cello, the gentle gliding bass: It's over. The bad boy's going now. It was the pity on her face. If only it had been contempt, or anger, or fury even. But no: pity. "Donald, why are you drinking again? You promised. You shouldn't do that with the anti-depressives. You've got to teach tonight. Donald?") the wonder of sirens and voices and human touch, the saving voices ("You'll be okay, sir." "I did it on purpose. I don't want to live." Ninety miles an hour, no seatbelt, the moment, the moment: "Now, God damn it!" That's it. Then the blackout. What happened next? How'd I live? Point four-oh. "You'll be okay, sir." Oh shit. "We'll take care of you, sir." The tree he aimed for still stood, his driver's side mirror lay splintered somewhere near it.)

The helpless resurrection. Death somehow thwarted. The ascension into life, the pain of rehab, the agony of self-confrontation, the vanquishing of the poisons, their resolute resistance, their hot screeching expulsion.

That alto again. The tenor listening, then starting anew down a lovely passage. At peace now, at home in the mountain range, the world, free to love again, he marveled at the cleanness of his feeling. If only Claire…

A quarter hour later Donald Helderman walks briskly along the campus of the college where he used to teach, energized by the workout, limber and smooth. Young people abound in the early afternoon sunlight. Some greet him as he glides past, he smiles and nods to each, happy to see them, wondering if any of his former students will be among them. It's been only a year since his retirement; there have to be some of his people still around here. It's almost one o'clock. He looks forward to his meeting today. It's been a good day so far, and he knows things will continue to get better. He'll be pleased to tell them so at the meeting. Now, if only Claire…

"Well hi, Dr. Helderman."

He turns at the sound of the voice, musical as a bird's. "Well…" He hesitates, searching for a name. His face brightens as he remembers. "Well, hi Melissa. So good to see you." His eyes swerve to her companion, a tall young man with thick curly hair and serious eyes. "And, um, Jeremy. Good to see you."

Jeremy extends his hand and Donald shakes it, then Melissa's. "How are you two doing?"

"We're doing fine, Dr. Helderman," Melissa says, and Jeremy nods. "We miss you around here."

"Well, thank you very much. You're very kind."

"Are you enjoying your retirement?" Jeremy asks.

A flood of feelings and images—it's been a long, deep year—inundate Donald's head and leave him momentarily unguarded, but he dams them up and smiles. "I love it," he says. "Every minute of it."

His former students laugh. "That's great, Dr. Helderman," Melissa says. "What are you doing with all your time?"

"Oh, the usual retirement things. A lot of reading and writing. Working out. Socializing. Some volunteer things."

"Travel?" asks Jeremy.

"That's in the future," Donald says. "I'm looking forward to that, but not yet."

He wants to leave, to get to his meeting, but as he speaks with these students, these children, he sees fondness in their eyes, their smiles.

"Do you miss teaching, Dr. Helderman?"

His eyes linger on Melissa's pale, bony face with its crimson lips and heavily mascaraed eyes, her long black hair. "You know," he says, "I always loved teaching, loved being in the classroom." The students look at him with the anticipation of a lecture on Socrates or on Nietzsche. "But now I look at retirement as a new career. I want to do a good job of it. I figure I've got a good twenty-five years to become good at it."

"That's really cool," says Melissa, as if hearing a revelation.

"I just think of the students who won't have you during that time," Jeremy says. "I feel bad for them."

Donald studies him, smiles gently, offers a little bow. "Why, thank you very much," he says. "I'll carry that thought with me."

These two, among the favorites of his ten thousand former students, those rather uncommon ones scattered along the periphery of convention, those who have known the quivering of life on the edge, who have found comfort in their whiskey and their marijuana and who slip into their lovemaking as into the consolation of a hot bath, students like himself at that age who haven't yet determined which of the proffered paths they'd follow, mainstream, margin, or perdition, and who couldn't yet know that either of the first two alternatives might entail the third—these two stood out during the last semester he taught, before the big crash and his abrupt retirement. He watches them walk away, Melissa with her little bandy legs and Jeremy, all shuffling jeans and heavy hair, and he feels a moment's nostalgia floating on Mark O'Connor's strings in his head and he stands beneath the campus maples smiling benignly.

He folds his hands and draws them up to his lips and listens for a moment to the music in his head, then remembers his watch and sees that he's late for his meeting. It started ten minutes ago, too late, despite the other members' tolerance, to open the door and disturb their preliminary readings. Besides that, he doesn't want to disturb his own musings. He finds a bench nestled amid fully blossomed purple lilacs and sits, rests his arm on the back and crosses his legs, his head down, listening to his breathing, his breath caressed by the lilacs. Can I teach again? he asks himself. He looks up and his eyes focus on a small granite monument in the form of an open book, a font protruding from it with a seated scholar dispensing a stream of water from his mouth into a clear pool. He smiles, raises his eyes to the canopy of blooming maples, clusters of yellow seeds still waiting for a breeze to loosen them, listens to the robins, smells the life of the city.

Can I...can I make love again?

He closes his eyes, follows his breath for its sounds in his nose, its cadences, its elasticity.

Can I love again? he asks.

Slowly he shakes his head.

No, he thinks, I can't teach again. I'll never do that again. He surveys the students in the distance lolling on the deep green lawn, congregating near the steps of the large utilitarian classroom building, walking easily the campus paths. He searches for the Melissas and Jeremys among them, the ones who always seemed to find one another in their loneliness and their gentle urgency, their curiosity and creativity, who always sat near each other in class and would approach him after lectures or in his office to offer friendly questions respectfully and to listen as though his replies meant something. You can distinguish them pretty easily, he thinks, in their gliding unconventionality, their envelope of gentle narcissism. He smiles, gives up the search.

Nope, that's over, he thinks. Over and done with. Along with a lot of other things: the bottle in his office cabinet, the other one in his briefcase, the deception, the increasing isolation, the solipsism, the betrayal of his profession and his colleagues, the growing impatience with his students. The intimidation of Claire, the browbeating, the contempt. And gone too, with his treatment and recovery, was his entire past, his life as a living entity, as a palpable presence, the whole inexorable path leading to his suicide attempt—Jesus, ninety miles an hour without a seatbelt, a four-oh alcohol level: he should have died just from that. The tree shearing off his outer mirror, a foot away from his head. Jesus!

The whole shebang—gone. Done for. Kaput. Except, of course,

as a memory, a memento, a long filmic chronicle as meaningful but as impersonal as any stranger's autobiography. And good riddance, too, he thinks. It's all new now, a new start, I'm in good health, everything is pure potentiality now. His eyes stray to the heavy Romanesque church down the street, the site of the meeting he had planned to attend where he can envision his fellow addicts in various stages of dealing with their afflictions, either sharing fragments of their shattered lives or simply bullshitting their way through court orders or making half-hearted stabs at pleasing somebody else, a spouse or a lover, a weeping parent.

Suddenly the last of his questions springs up again, vexatious and saddening both: Can I love again? His dreams, on the few occasions when he recalls them, are of whiskey not Claire. His kids are spread out, distant and ashamed, too angry to tell their own children about him. And Claire. Moved away. A full-time resident of their summer home an hour away, a stranger to him now, driven away to find herself and regain her own sanity. Claire. Can I even love her again? And then, can I make love again?

Not fuck, like the sodden nights. Make love.

Claire.

I've got to call her, he decides. He's not supposed to, he knows, not for another three days, twice a week is all, but he's got to call her now. It's imperative. He holds off, a motorcycle sputters at a traffic light, then roars away. Pigeons coo softly nearby. He hears honking, he hears voices, he hears squealing brakes. Finally he smiles tight-lipped and broadly, nods his head with unrestrained vigor, springs up and pulls his cell phone from his pocket. He's going to do it.

His hands shake as he strains to remember her number. Cell

phone, not cottage. He fidgets and dances like a boy with a full bladder, poking the air with a free finger. He flips open the phone and taps an assortment of tiny buttons, knits his brow and stares at the blank screen and shakes the little instrument, his body beating a wild, barely controlled rhythm, like subway drumming on plastic pails. Then it stops, he throws his head back, his mouth opens with a mute exclamation of discovery, his head drops back down. He presses the on button.

"Be there, Claire," he says aloud as he taps out her number again. "Be there, babe. Please be there, babe. Please be there." His body gyrates and he begins to pace. He stops when after the fifth ring he hears Claire's smooth alto voice.

"Claire?" he says

"Donnie?" Her voice almost stumbles over his.

"Claire? Um, it's me." He hears a silence and then a loud exhalation, probably of smoke.

"Why are you calling, Donnie? You're not supposed to call. We just talked yesterday."

He begins to pace again, creating a trail on the unmowed spring grass.

"I need to talk with you."

"You're not supposed to call for three more days."

"I need to hear your voice, Claire."

"You heard it yesterday."

"I need to hear it every day, Claire." He walks on dappled grass to the trunk of an enormous oak.

"You used to hear it all the time, and you never once listened to it."

He leans against the rough bark, his body shivering.

"I'm going nuts alone, Claire."

"I went nuts with you, Don."

His eyes shut, his eyebrows arch as his head tilts back. He holds his breath.

"Donald?"

"Claire," he says, his voice thin. "Think of all the history."

"The history haunts me, Don."

He winces. His posture is unchanged.

"But Claire? That's past. That's all in the past."

"Not for me, Don." She hesitates. "It's way too much alive. It's right in front of me, Don. Right in your voice."

"But Claire, you can't believe how hard I'm working," he says, eyes wide open now, glaring at his loneliness. "Everything's changed for me. I'm working on this thing every day."

"Good. Keep working, Don. So will I."

"Can I see you, Claire?"

"No, Don. You can't see me. Not now."

"But Claire… "

"I don't want to see you, Don. Get that into your head."

"Claire."

"No, Don. Someday."

He folds the little instrument, places it in his jacket pocket, inhales deeply, closes his eyes. Above him in the oak a squirrel grumbles and he looks up, flooded with hurt. Verdant Appalachian hillsides are far distant now, there never was a civilly playful exchange with a pleasant professional woman in a downtown café a few hours ago, the lovely vulnerable students lamenting his loss to a future generation have dematerialized like last winter's snow. His mind empty, he stares numbly at a trembling hand, its uneven nails, its bushy knuckles, he looks around and begins slowly walking in the direction of the brilliant Romanesque edifice down the street from the campus. Sunlight and shadow play lively games on its broad brick face and portals and its roseate window, attracting him to a meeting inside that must be nearly finished. He gets about twenty paces away from the oak and stops. He reaches into his pocket for the cell phone and extracts it. He gazes at it and squeezes it tightly in his hand, turns and faces the oak. He takes a few steps toward the tree and suddenly hurls the silvery implement with a startling fierceness, sees it strike the broad trunk and carom off to the side but doesn't see it land and skid, hears the squirrel chatter and rustle somewhere in the tree's lower crown. He turns away and bends down and clutches his knees.

Sensing the flight of time in the dance of shadows around him, Donald twists his head rather than his arm to read his watch. He spreads his legs apart, hands still on his knees, then leans far down and touches the end of each shoe with his fingertips. His body rocks imperceptibly as he holds that position before straightening his torso, keeping his legs apart. He stretches his arms sideways and holds his head up to the sunlight, bows slowly and twists and extends his left arm to his right foot. Former students and students who will never have him for a class watch the limber old man admiringly. Those who saw him hurl his cell phone think about calling the campus police. Donald Helderman listens to Mark O'Connor gracefully moving to his major 7th finale, hoping for some new love.

RACCOON REDUX

The boy Chris hadn't slept well in the small two person dome tent, curled up on the floor in his sleeping bag with his lanky Uncle Richard, two knapsacks, and a cooler. His uncle didn't snore, but he murmured every so often, and upon hearing the garbled voice the boy would strain to imagine what interesting episode from the man's life he was commenting on, and whether he was going to say anything sexy or in any other way interesting.

For that matter, Chris had experienced some difficulty in keeping his own mind quiet, what with the memories of his first caresses of a girl's leg, Karen's, pretty as a grown up's, her skin sleek as a glossy photograph, her thigh, her thigh, ah her thigh, the texture of peanut butter. From vivid recollection to active imagination being an infinitesimal step for a twelve year old, images of Victoria Secret breasts and hips flooded his head and his hyperalert penis with waves of ecstatic pulsations, though he knew, of course, that Karen wasn't yet possessed of such wonders. Still, she had pretty, sleek, and tanned legs, and he had touched them, caressed them, and who knows? In a year or two those legs might lead to those other things, and …who knows?

But it wasn't only his uncle's gravelly mumbling and the wonders of his fanciful early adolescent sensuality that had kept him awake most of the night. Nor could he attribute his sleep deprivation to the dry ground that the tent floor and his sleeping bag did nothing to soften, though that too was part of the problem. No, the main source of his sleeplessness was the passing alongside the tent of the nighttime critters, the snoops, the tireless wanderers, the inveterate foragers and scavengers, probably raccoons but maybe skunks too, some of whom had the temerity to poke and sniff and breathe near his head, sometimes rubbing along the tent's thin nylon skin and consequently along his back or arm, whichever was touching the wall in the confines of that space too crowded for even Chris to easily crawl around in. If his annoyance with those little furry guys hadn't kept him in a state of alarmed wakefulness, the image of Karen's legs might have been confined to sweet dreams and his uncle's growls to the domain of perpetual silence.

And the sight that confronted him at five forty-five in the gathering dawn under the canopy of beech limbs wouldn't be holding him in the thrall of pity. And terror.

So this is what raised his hackles just a short time ago, woke Uncle Richard too: the terrifying screeching, the sounds of flailing mortality. Paralyzed with chills at first, he had, once the din ceased, followed an impulse to drag his uncle out of the sack to help him find the source of the noise and they had followed a trail two hundred yards under the guidance of flashlights and Chris had been the first to see the carnage.

Unable to take his eyes off the mangled animal, the boy's desire to run was thwarted by his fascination with the grim spoilage. "Uncle Richard," he said.

"Yeah?"

"Over here."

He heard the dead leaf shuffle of hiking boots on the messy forest floor, the crackling of dried twigs. He saw his uncle's legs standing beside him, heard the whisper, "Jesus."

The boy stared hard. "I guess that's what made the noise, huh?" he said.

"I guess so. What a beating he took."

"Yeah. What a mess."

Uncle Richard crouched down. "Look." He pointed to a mild disturbance in the air just above the raccoon's torso. "See the heat rising?" The boy nodded. "He's still warm. He's not been dead more than a few minutes."

Chris raised his head, directed his gaze to the small patches of sky visible through the treetops. He was blinking rapidly. "I know. I heard all the noise."

Uncle Richard stood and placed a hand on the boy's shoulder. The boy sniffed once, then several more times rapidly. "I can smell the blood," he said. "It smells like what I've tasted, only stronger even." He looked down at the carcass, left the site and returned with a long gnarled stick. He tried to turn the carcass, managed only a nudge before the stick broke. "Heavy," he said. He looked up at his tall uncle and asked if he could maybe touch the fur.

"Sure," his uncle said gently.

Chris squatted, reached out a tentative finger, touched the fur on the top of the head, on the ear. Lying on its side, the raccoon's open eye stared at nothing and the boy touched it too. After withdrawing his finger, he hesitated a moment before touching the little teeth in its open mouth, caught in a mute final snarl of pain. He didn't say anything. Then he touched the fur matted with its rapidly drying fluids, withdrew his hand and studied his red fingers, rubbed them together, smelled them. "Can I touch its guts?" he asked.

"Go ahead."

He touched it the way he had first touched Karen's calf, her ankle bone, the tendons behind her knee, with great reserve, with great care, like a pianist touching the keys of the first piano he's seen after a month of starvation in a desert. It seemed to him strange and mysterious to feel this warm, smooth, rubbery thing, this vital thing, this thing hidden inside a body that contributed to the livingness, the functionality of this creature, now so useless, so inert, so meaningless. He shifted his feet a bit, rested his arms on his knees, his hands dangling. Flies were beginning to gather, to land on the nose, the gums, the drying flesh, the first of the scavengers to begin nature's work. He stood up, buried his hands in his pockets, raised his eyes, rapidly blinking again, and scanned the forest. A single snort, a suppressed sob, escaped him and he used the back of his hand to wipe a tear from his cheek. His uncle reached around and drew him against his side.

"Uncle Richard?" he said.

"Hmm?"

The boy returned his hand to his pocket. "Why... Why do people feel so bad when an animal gets all wrecked and killed like this?"

Uncle Richard studied the boy with raised eyebrows. He clenched his jaw, pursed his lips. "I suppose, um, because it's life,

Chris." He hesitated. "It's life gone. You know, it was a life and now the life is gone. Zapped. Kaput. Vacant."

The boy looked up at him. "Yeah, but it's only an animal."

"Mm hmm. But it used to be a live animal. And cute, right? Raccoons are cute, don't you think?"

"Yeah. But he's sure not cute anymore."

"See? He was a cute little guy, full of life, before. Now death has made him grotesque, ugly. Do you think he wanted to be grotesque and ugly? And dead?"

Chris smiled. "No. Not at all."

"Do you think he still wanted to be alive and cute?"

"Sure."

"Do you think all living things want to stay alive and be cute? Maybe even forever?"

"Sure they do. Except maybe flies. They could never be cute."

"True, true. But I'll bet they want to live. Just like the raccoon. Just like you."

"Yes."

The boy watched as the flies zipped around on the carcass. He listened to the waft of birdsong, the calls of distant geese, smelled bacon on the breeze. "Do you think he suffered a lot?"

Uncle Richard nodded, pursed his lips again. "I expect so. It must have been pretty bad."

"Uncle Richard?"

"Yeah Chris."

"How come people don't feel as bad when people get wrecked and killed like they do when animals do?"

"What makes you think they don't, Chris?"

"Well, it seems that it's in all the movies and TV and everything. People are always hurting and killing people, and people who watch all that stuff think it's cool. And it's always on television, and in my comic books. And my games. It seems like people really think it's cool to kill people, but they feel bad when animals get killed. I can't figure it out."

Uncle Richard stepped in front of the boy and grasped both his shoulders. "You know what, Chris? Neither can I." He drew the boy to him and embraced him, then stepped back, his eyes holding on to the boy's. He shook his head. "I sure can't either…Come on," he said. "Let's get back to camp. We'll have a bite to eat and then go fishing."

Chris gave a farewell glance to the rapidly cooling carcass and joined his uncle. "I don't think I want to go fishing," he said.

"You don't? Why not? That's what we came here to do."

"Maybe later. I'm really tired. I didn't sleep much last night. Can I just get in my sleeping bag and go to sleep for a while?'

Uncle Richard threw his arms around the boy's shoulders. "Sure," he said. "You take a snooze and I'll go throw a line in and wake you up in two hours. Okay?"

"Sure. Thanks." He smiled and held the smile the rest of the way to his campsite. He was able to hold the smile so long because as he trod through the ferns and old leaves and broken sticks of that tamed state forest his mind was on Karen, she of the smooth skin and the soft lips, she of the peanut butter thighs and the sweet fingers on his face, and he thought of what he was going to do under the cover of his sleeping bag with only her image to excite him.

BLACKIE'S SAD NIGHT

Holy Christ! ...Char, come here a minute." Blackie Jaskiewicz had just leapt from his easy chair, slamming his hands against his forehead and latching onto it as if to keep it from crumbling. When his wife heard his cry she dropped the pan she was wiping and rushed to the den and found him in that pose of desperation, his eyes stretched wide and his lower jaw hanging as if broken and limp. As she entered the room he pointed to the television and she turned in alarm as the news event of the evening was being rerun.

"Jesus, Char," Blackie shouted. "Watch this. It's awful. It's just awful."

Char's slender fingertips met at her lips and her eyes took on the look of helpless anticipation as the sequence progressed in living color. What she saw was a playful looking heavyset older man astraddle a huge loping Hereford bull waving his cowboy hat wildly in the air in imitation of a rodeo Brahma rider and wearing a hearty grin. Abruptly the bull stops bucks and twists, then runs about twenty yards and stops again. The heavy man flies through the air, his hat popping off to reveal a bald head with white trim. Char takes in a loud breath and Blackie cries, “Oh my God.” The old man lands on his shoulder and face, crumples and rolls and slides forward and comes to a stop face down. His body seems to crimp, his hips and thighs rising and his knees pressing downward at an angle, then it relaxes and lies still. The panicked bull is seen in the background running crazily. He stops, eyes the man on the ground, and charges. “Oh no!” cries Char as the bull approaches and tramples the body, runs on and turns and treads on the body again. A later broadcast in slow motion will reveal the bull losing its balance slightly as one of its forehooves slides off the man’s thigh. For a moment the old man lies motionless, then he slowly struggles to rise as the camera zooms in faster than it can focus clearly. “Oh Jesus Christ,” moans Blackie. The man stands with unrecognizable face, a face that doesn’t look human, his blue, red, and yellow checkered shirt and brown corduroys torn and one arm dangling and waving, he reels, almost falls, staggers for two steps, and, arms at his sides, his entire body from face to knees hitting at once like a felled log, he falls face down again in the hard, barren dirt. The camera angle shoots upward past treetops to the azure sky as if the shooter had lost control, then descends and searches, finds the body, and refocuses. The man lies almost still. His arm moves, then his leg, then he seizes and Blackie moans again, invokes his God again, and suddenly we see a massive white head bovine and curly haired and bedecked with glinting horns that look metallic on the screen approach the prone body at full gallop and we see and can actually feel the silent crushing thump of the blow, Char emits a cry and Blackie, his hands having slid up over and back down his head and now grasping the nape of his neck, shouts out "Holy Jesus Christ almighty" as the body rises like a thick lump of dough and flies for several feet as if bone and muscle had never thought of inhabiting it and it hits the ground and bounces twice, slides, and settles. "Bobby Horstphal, dead at sixty-nine, doing what he loved most: putting on the entertainment at his godson's high school graduation party," says the pretty local newscaster, whose smooth young face and golden hair has replaced the dead man's body on the screen. Abruptly her face disappears, replaced instantly by a number of young women sitting around a swimming pool in which bobs a floating beer can the size of a tanker trailer on end.

"Jesus, Char," Blackie Jaskiewicz shouted. "Did you see what I just saw? Jesus Christ, what did I just see?"

Char turned to him, both her hands cupped over her mouth, her shoulders hunched. She slowly shook her head. "Did you know him?" she asked.

"No. No. No I didn't know him. No, but it doesn't make any difference, does it? Oh Jesus, it's horrible." Under ordinary circumstances his volume would have been inappropriately loud. He dropped his hands and trod a path through the dining area and into the kitchen and back several times until the series of commercials was over, then stopped next to Char, who was rearranging a bouquet of lilacs on the fireplace mantel. "Oh no! Look." This time his baritone voice cracked. "Another repeat."

She turned to see the bull approach the body, this time in slow motion, the massive head of the beast, as large as a desktop and solid as a wrecking ball, turned slightly, the crown lowering, horns glistening, its eye fixed on the prone object before it, then the impact, Char's breath abrading her throat in terror, Blackie crying out, cursing, "Oh Jesus fucking Christ, oh no," the w-o-o-mp that could be felt if not heard, the limp body looking like an inflated meat casing rising from the ground, limbs flailing momentarily before landing in slow motion still, the shot sufficiently close-up for Blackie and Char to see the shoulder separate from its left outstretched arm as it took the full weight of the fall, then the side of the head hit and dribble on the hard dirt as the body twisted and the chest and abdomen hit and finally the legs, bouncing and landing again, and then an abrupt shot change to a close-up of an old man, heavier than the dead one, his face craggy and sad, for he had been weeping.

"With us in the studio is Bobby Horstphal's longtime friend and companion Warren Monday, who this afternoon witnessed this horrible scene." The offscreen voice was that of the newswoman, who spoke solemnly. Char and Blackie stood stationary in front of their television, still in an attitude of shock. "Mr. Monday, what led to Mr. Horstphal's getting on that bull today?"

The bust of Warren Monday filled Blackie and Char's large screen TV, his heavy face large-pored and jowly, his nose like a russet potato. He closed his eyes before he spoke, took in two short breaths, folded his thick hands.

"Well, Bobby liked riding bulls," he answered. His gravelly voice betrayed a longtime smoking habit. His chin nestled deep in the fat of his neck, he spoke with downcast eyes. "He used to ride them in rodeos years ago. But this wasn't supposed to be a bustin' competition. Bobby quit that years ago. And Ivan..."—he pronounced the name Eevon—"was like his pet. Why, he was on Ivan's back a couple of times a week, just for fun. And because he loved that bull."

"But what was the occasion that brought out this mock bull ride today, Mr. Monday?" the interviewer asked, leaning forward with deep concern.

Warren Monday's interlocked fingers seemed completely at rest, but when he answered the question his voice cracked. "Why, he was pretending he was in a rodeo for the kids. It was his godson's ninth birthday, and he and his friends were out for the day. Them and their daddies and mommies. And a bunch of neighbor folks." The voice stopped and the camera slowly zoomed forward to study the subject's brows working like storm clouds, his cheeks twitching like slowly buckling pavement. "Aw," he whined, "Bobby was so happy when he made the kiddies laugh."

A sudden switch to the second camera caught the interviewer close up gently biting her lips. She glanced into the camera and folded her lips between her teeth and nodded. "You and Bobby were long-time friends, weren't you?"

The second camera zoomed slightly back to a medium shot of them both as Warren Monday answered. "Fifty-seven years," he said, his eyes unfocused. "Since we was twelve years old." He hesitated for a poignant moment. "See, we was lovers for fifty-five of those years." The first camera returned to a close up of Warren Monday's face, eyes open now but gazing downward to the left. The newswoman's voice repeated the word "lovers" as a gasping question. "Jesus Christ!" said Blackie. "What!" Char exclaimed.

"Holy shit," Blackie bellowed. "Did you hear that?"

"Yes I did." Char looked at her husband as though he told her that their baby had been hit by a car. Then she returned to the TV screen. A commercial for gum had replaced the interview.

"Those old farts are queer." Blackie stared at the commercial without seeing it. What he saw was in his mind: a replay of Bobby Horstphal struggling to his feet, arm dangling uselessly, staggering, then falling flat, his face hitting the packed dirt simultaneous with his chest, the old man, the old man. Dying there, in front of Blackie's eyes. In his mind.

"I can't believe what we're seeing," said Blackie. "Can you believe this?" His eyes seemed to grasp for Char, they implored, they reached for her like a flailing child in a pool.

"What's going on?" she said. "Blackie. I've never seen you like this."

"I mean, can you believe what's happening?" he moaned. "What we're seeing on this god damned television set?" He looked at the screen. An edited segment showed the bull running over the quivering body, sending its limbs into a flurry of movement. Then the newscaster's familiar voice and face returned, both solemn, astonished.

"We're back with Warren Monday in the WKBS studio in a tribute to his friend and lover, Bobby Horstphal, who was killed by a berserk pet bull during a party at the men's farm outside of Sparta today…"

"Tribute?" said Blackie. "This is a tribute? Bullshit. This is an exploitation. It's an exploitation of a guy's weird way to be killed and these old guys who are queer for a story, to get the viewers tuned in, that's all it is."

Char shushed him and they turned their attention to the image of the newscaster, her legs crossed, a pad of paper on her lap and a pencil poised in her hand, and the heavy old man slumped in the small chair beside her, his head, couched in its cushions of neck fat, shaking "no" back and forth rhythmically, subtly, almost imperceptibly.

"Mr. Monday, you said that you and Bobby Horstphal were partners for fifty-seven years? That's a long time."

Warren Monday's eyes looked up though his head remained tilted downward. His brows jumped upward as if startled into some sort of epiphany. "Yes, it is," he said.

"And you...you shared your life together all that time?"

Raising his head, his face took on a new look, relaxed, he smiled, seemed eager to talk, as if happy that someone wanted to know about him. "Well, we ran off together at sixteen," he said. "Went to Wyoming, Cheyenne. We liked that name..." He continued to talk but his voice became background sound as another voice intruded.

"Yo, Blackie. Am I the first one here?"

"Shit," Blackie said, turning away from the TV. The screen door slammed and he saw the beaming face of his friend Dougie, a six pack of beer in one hand and a plastic sandwich bag full of coins in the other.

"I'm going next door, check on the boys, chat a little while with Diane," Char said. "Say hi to all the guys. Have fun tonight, Blackie. Okay?" She kissed him, called a greeting to Dougie, and went through the kitchen. Blackie heard the back door close, turned to the TV to see Warren Monday slowly gesturing to a grinning interviewer, heard some disconnected words, and felt a hand on his shoulder.

"I see you're watching the news. Too bad about that faggot, huh Blackie? Jesus, what a god-awful thing. Hey, you got the table all set up? I've got a good feeling about tonight."

"All set up, my friend," Blackie answered. Tall and lean, with the face of an ebullient hunting dog, Dougie held up his six pack. "You can put it in the fridge downstairs," Blackie told him. "Go ahead down. I'll be down in a second or two." As Dougie clambered down the uncarpeted stairway to the rec room where the table waited for him laden with chips and salsa, dishes with an assortment of cheeses and cold sausage slices, beer cups and plastic dishes and colorful napkins, Blackie scribbled a note instructing the other expected penny-ante gamblers to come on in and go on down, then taped it to the front door. On his way back across the living room he stopped in front of the TV.

"Guess I'll have to do it on my own now," he saw Warren Monday say. The old man's creased, heavy face was somber again.

"Do what?" asked the interviewer.

"Get on livin'," Warren Monday replied. The camera zoomed in as he looked inside himself, shaking his head in profound perplexity.

"Gonna be a long time alone," he said.

"Aw Jesus," said Blackie. "Aw fuck."

He raised his hand to his face, covered his mouth with it, his index finger pressing against the septum of his nose as if to stifle a sneeze. He closed his eyes, took a breath, opened them to see Bobby Horstphal flying and landing and being trampled as background to the credits for the news production.

• • • •

"That guy Ben Wallace, I never seen a man play like him," said Dougie, his eyes glued to the basketball game on the flat television screen on the wall rather than on the hand that held his playing cards. Other than the junkyard section of piled toys in one corner, the cheerfully lit room was orderly, manly. Golf knick-knacks and posters of blue water bordering lush green fairways, along with mounted freshwater fish and a shelf lined with autographed baseballs, conveyed a congenial sportsman's disposition. It was a room Blackie was proud of, a room where he could withdraw after a difficult shift at the plant and play with his two young sons or work a jigsaw puzzle with the TV tuned to a ball game or hockey match, or, with its wet bar and small refrigerator, entertain his friends over cards and beer.

"You in the game or not?" The dealer's voice had an edge to it. "Come on, man, you play cards or watch the fucking game."

"I'm in." Dougie tossed a dime into the pot of mostly shiny coins. "Gimme three."

Blackie drew three also, glanced at them, dropped all his cards face down. "I'm out," he said. "James, next time deal me something to play with, okay?"

"Damn right, Blackie. I'll deal you a new dick, that's what I'll deal you. You can play with that all the rest of the night, sucker."

"Only in the other room, okay pardner?" added Terry through his overgrown walrus mustache. "I got enough to put up with with these obscene cards James deals me. I don't need to watch no sodomy between you and yourself on top of it."

"At least Brother Blackie won't be diddlin' no over the hill rodeo farmer in that other room," James observed.

"Right on," agreed Terry. "That sorry old faggot is sure as hell dead, ain't he. I wonder if the other guy is going to start buggering that bull now."

Blackie abruptly stood. "Excuse me, guys. I gotta go make use of that other room right now."

"Aha, you can't wait till my next deal, huh Blackie?" laughed James. "We done got you all hot and bothered right now."

Without answering Blackie crossed the room and entered the small bathroom. He closed the door a bit too loudly and stood in the dark. He squeezed his eyes shut and gritted his teeth and the Hereford's enormous head loomed in his brain, its feathery facial hair rippling as the monolithic, infrangible head grew larger, more fearsome, more terrifyingly lethal. And then he saw it hit that body, closer up and in slower motion than the camera caught it, the body like a flimsy dummy stuffed with tissue except that you could feel the impact, the resistance, however minor, that the two hundred and fifty pound torso offered the indomitable force of the massive animal, and you could feel the weight at the moment the body collided with the immovable dirt before it bounced and slid and lay still.

Blackie held himself up by clutching the sink, leaned over, let his head sag. It was the first time he ever felt like crying.

He had cried before, twice, once at his father's funeral mass and once when his first-born boy had been brought back to life after a near drowning in a neighbor's pool. *Jason. Hair like sunshine, face smooth as milk glass. Limp and dead. Poor guy, poor little guy. Limp as a dead eel. And then alive. Alive. Jesus Christ, alive!* Each time the emotion had exploded unannounced, unplanned, a riot of sound and a geyser of tears, leaving him exhausted, confused, helpless. And there were times when he had been near to crying but had stifled the impulse before the eyes could leak a single telltale droplet. A man is a man, after all, even when a boy, even when scared or lonely or hurt. But now he felt like crying. He wanted to cry. For the first time.

Gonna be a long time alone. Jesus, he whispered.

Back at the table he took some kidding for not flushing the toilet, and there followed some clever bathroom humor that even silent Gil, who hadn't uttered a word about faggots or bestiality during the earlier exchange that drove Blackie away from the table, contributed to as he shuffled and dealt the cards. For a time the evening went smoothly, pleasantly, with no one winning or losing excessively and with occasional cheering at outstanding play by the Pistons on TV. And though the empty beer cans added up and a few shots of whiskey were downed by Dougie and Terry, no one seemed more than mellow, certainly not louder than normal, nor disrespectful of the sleeping children upstairs. Blackie liked these evenings of nickel-dime poker with his friends, liked the coarseness and playfulness of his buddies, whom he would see again in just a few hours back at the plant, but that was all right, sometimes he just couldn't get enough of them. And then the basketball game was over, the time to call last hand was drawing near, and Blackie looked up to see Bobby Horstphal flying through the air and landing on his shoulder as a male voice-over announced the tragedy and invited the viewing audience to stay tuned for the eleven o'clock news, coming up soon.

A panicky feeling arose in Blackie like when he had to address an audience, a city commission or a union cell. Like way back in school when he was unexpectedly called on to recite a sequence of events in history class. The flushing, the terrible adrenalin rush pounding his chest, the short choppy breathing.

"Jesus, again?" said Dougie. "Haven't they overplayed this thing enough?"

Terry, who had been shuffling, looked up with a glare. "Fuck," he growled. "I'm fucking sick of that old fucking faggot and this whole fucking news program."

Blackie studied him. Oddly, as he listened to Terry rant, he felt himself relax. He slouched in his chair, listened to the stream of aspersions, undammed and torrential, rushing from the mouths of his friends, at least three of them. Silent Gil just remained silent, sipping his beer, nodding slightly with a slight ambiguous smirk. The game evidently over, Blackie sank further into his chair, raised his arms and clasped his hands behind his head. The room—what was the word? he thought. Appointed. That's it. Nicely appointed. It was a man's room: the oak paneling, the baseball lined shelf, the wood and leather framed photo of the grizzled fisherman netting a trout in the rapids of a northern stream, the mounted brown trout and largemouth bass, the golf paraphernalia, the wet bar, it was all there, complete, his maleness made manifest in this room, the whole environment a vital bequest to his boys whose playthings were piled in a corner.

His boys. Jason. Jason the miracle. Withdrawn now, removed from the dense hatred around him, Blackie smiled. Water gathered in his eyes, almost leaked out. Jason brought back to life. And precious Tony. Their toys. Their life. Abruptly he had a strange new thought. What if one of them turned out to be gay? What if both …He didn't hesitate. Shaking his head slightly, he became aware of a new, unanticipated idea, a renunciation of sorts, an unqualified denial: Nothing, *no thing*, would ever come between him and his boys. Nothing. Never. First comes love, he thought. That's first. Nothing else matters. Then as the TV screen took shape again, a new idea struck him as he saw the camera move toward Warren

Monday's face. And grief, he thought. Love and grief. They come first. After them, nothing else matters.

He scanned his room once more and settled on the TV screen. Warren Monday was talking in a close up, he strained to hear but caught only phrases between his friends' loud sneers and jests. Something about a violation, out there in Wyoming, he being forced to watch while Bobby was violated by some cowboys in a corral or someplace. "Ha!" James laughed. "I bet they got a donkey into his ass." That started the whooping, the hysterics. "Hey, donkey, ass—ass, donkey!" Dougie shouted. "Good one," hollered Terry. "They go together like smoke up a chimbley. A donkey into a queer's ass."

Must stop them, Blackie thought. Got to stop them. I don't need this shit. Not any more. He was feeling hatred smoldering. "Hey Terry," he shouted above the uproar. "Hey Terry." When he got the other's attention, he lowered his voice. "How many years you been married, my friend?" he asked.

"You mean me?" Terry asked.

Smiling, Blackie glanced at the others, suddenly hushed, then returned to Terry with a wink.

"You know as well as I do, Blackie. Four years."

"This time," said Blackie.

"Yeah, this time."

"How long the last time?"

"You know. Eight years."

"And the first time."

"What you getting at, Blackie?"

"How many years the first time?"

"Two."

"That's fourteen years altogether. With three wives. How old are you, Terry?"

"Thirty eight. What you getting at, Blackie?"

"Why, Terry, can't you see?" Gil, the quiet one, said. "Those guys on TV were together fifty-five years. Fifty-five years. Sixty-nine years old."

"So? What the fuck?" He stopped. His face suddenly took on the appearance of having figured out a sinister truth. He cocked his head and leered first at Blackie then at Gil. "Shee. You gonna tell me you two are faggot lovers? You gonna tell me that?"

Gil placed both hands on the table and pushed himself upright. He towered over everybody when they all stood together, but now as they sat he seemed a youthful Titan. He buried his powerful hands in his jeans pockets and turned his gaze to the textured ceiling not far above his head and pursed his mouth as if deep in thought. Then he looked down at Terry. "Hey Terry," he said. "Did you ever tell these guys why your second wife divorced you?" He glared hard at Terry, his voice deep as a well. "So okay. I'll tell them. She said she divorced you because she said you thought the only way you could make a kid was by coming into her ass."

No one laughed or even smirked. All eyes fastened on Terry's change of color, the protrusion of his jaw muscle. James leaned over and clamped his hand on Terry's arm. "See Terry?" he said. "You see what's happened? Now what do you want to say a thing like that for, Fool?" he asked. "You don't talk like that, not in this man's home."

Slouched in his chair, Blackie rested his elbow on its metal arm and supported his chin with his thumb, his index finger gently rubbing his lips. His outward peacefulness, his ease, his slow breathing somehow made him menacing as he stared at Terry. He was dealing with a violence inside. It was a violence born of memory, of long gone teenaged malice, of old tormenting sensations, of the popping sound of a jawbone breaking against the outer edge of his sledgelike fist as it arced back with lightning speed after the right cross had sent the victim's head ricocheting off his own shoulder, back in the gangster days of his youth, the days he was called Hammer, not Blackie. The dark days. The days he tried hard to forget. But now, at this buzzing moment of barely contained rage, he felt with alarming vividness the bones in Terry's face shatter with the same life-altering suddenness as his teenage adversary's, the hard meaty edge of his fist feeling not much more resistance than that offered by a maple leaf, and he saw Terry flop on the ground mewling like a muffled opossum in its death throes, just as that poor kid did, and then he saw just as clearly in his mind's eye the body of Bobby Horstphal, mute and helpless and dying, jouncing on the hard dirt under the sharp hooves of a two-thousand pound beast. Blackie closed his eyes. "The game's over, guys," he said. "Time to get outa here."

The last to leave was Gil who still stood motionless, looking down from a foot higher at Blackie's thick, wavy hair and its telltale sign of incipient shedding. "I'll crush the son of a bitch if you'd like, Blackie," he said. "He'll break like a twig in winter."

"No thanks, my man." Reaching up he patted Gil's shoulder. "No need to do that for me."

"I'll see you in the morning then."

Outside later, Blackie found himself mesmerized by stars, staring blankly over the black treetops, fantasizing Bobby Horstphal at sixty-nine busting the enormous Hereford bull in front of a hundred laughing children, arena dust swirling far upward to meet the distant cosmic debris performing its eternal dance invisibly and indefatigably out there now, somewhere. He again wanted to cry and he closed his eyes and tears leaked from behind his lids and coursed down his face and he felt glad, as though it were supposed to happen, as though the oozing fluid were a part of this rhythm he was feeling, this waltz with the heavens, this touch of some smooth new melody whose notes were forming for his ken alone. What brought this on? he wondered obliquely, this feeling unlike any he had experienced before, even when his boy had rejoined the living, and even when he and Char had come together again afterward in a frightening blast of agonized jubilation, of gasping relief. What brought this on?

But he knew, he knew. He knew and he was amazed. In mute exultation he slowly raised his cupped hands as if in prayer and extended them and then slowly brought them to his forehead, his eyes still closed, face to the stars. He sopped up the silence. He slid his fingers down over his eyes and cupped his lower face, his moist cheeks. *Gonna be a long time alone*, he heard Warren Monday lament.

A warm hand touched his back, an arm wrapped around his shoulder.

"Whatcha thinking about, Baby?" It was Char's twangy voice, soothing and melodious.

Blackie wiped his face, put an arm around his wife. "I never did learn those consolations up there," he said. "Those are consolations, aren't they?"

"Constellations. Con*stell*ations." She giggled.

"Con*stell*ations. I never did learn them. But if I'm not mistaken, one of them's a bull, isn't it?"

"Taurus, yes."

"Do you know where it is?"

"It's to the north, but you can't see it in the city. Too much glow from the lights down here. Why?"

Blackie took in a breath deeply. "I think I'd like to write a letter to Warren Monday. You know, the old guy whose lover got killed by that bull? Tell him to look up in the night sky at Taurus. See Bobby up there."

"I think that would be really nice," Char said

"I learned something today." His voice cracked. Char hadn't heard that before. She peered at his profile.

"I know." She watched his head nod slowly, pause, then tilt.

"It feels good," he said.

"Mm-hmm."

THE LITTLE BOY'S FULL BLADDER

Wouldn't it be something to be a bat, ugly little critter, flying smugly and with supreme disinterestedness in a shopping mall? Awake in the afternoon and therefore invisible because no one expects to see a flitting bat during the daylight hours, soaring and looping, darting, dropping and ascending haphazardly, in a hurry to get nowhere, observing everything with its sonar and its finely tuned nervous apparatus?

This bat of my imagination flies in wonder and amusement, free in the afternoon hubbub, small fleck against the enormous, glistening white openness of the mall, the only obstacles white walls and widely spaced wood columns reaching to the ceiling of the central atrium, minor interruptions of its otherwise carefree and unhurried excursion. To its acute sensoria all things are impressions immediate, intense, and solid. If they weren't, being blind it would forever suffer the thudding pain of headaches and broken wings from its encounters with the objects that it can't apprehend visually. But suppose it could see. And suppose that among the throngs of multicolored bipeds scurrying across the gleaming tiled floor below, amid the kiosks laden with wares from sneakers to wristwatches to cell phones and the leather furniture filled with slouching and snoozing forms and substances, standing out in the thick of monstrous amounts of merchandise and posters and words naming stores and brands, titles and eateries—among this almost infinite number of entities the bat spots a single boy standing alone, his head craned and following its flight with a look of open-mouthed awe. Wouldn't the bat, if it could see, find itself attracted to this boy of boys, this boy who alone found it in these daylight hours, who stands there investing in a feeling of fascination, with reverence almost? Might not the bat love the boy?

Or if love is too strong a word for this first-sight encounter, might not the bat at least zoom in on the boy, check him out, swoop down maybe and give him a thrill, give him his money's worth, as it were? Offer a little dollop of guano on his worn little sandal as an official greeting, a good natured calling card to show off to his mother, his buddies? If the bat had a sense of humor it might donate that little treat of its own making to the boy, or it might quickly fashion a makeshift nest in his hair; but at any rate, in its swift descent to inspect that smooth little face it would probably forget its intended prank upon glimpsing the cloud behind the boy's eyes, the bank of fog, dense enough to make any sensitive mammal, aloft or grounded, squirm and avert, retreat, flee. I'm not going too close to that mop of hair, it might decide. It's way too thick and tangly. Foggy eyes and snarled hair—man, I'm gone.

The bat vanishes and the boy stands frozen, eyes trained on the spot where he saw its last dip and rise. After a few moments he lowers his head and swivels it slowly, the eyes shifting now left and right, left and right, several times for each turn. He's looking for confirmation, for others also scanning the heights toward the skylights on the ceiling searching for the phantom bat, or else he's checking to see if others are gazing quizzically at him, wondering what his problem is, this boy with the craned neck, the arms doubled up and thumbs touching the corners of his mouth. But he sees only flashes of colors and churning legs, impersonal forms flowing past like currents and backwashes, so he puts his hands in his jean pockets and shuffles forward with a gait that signals that he doesn't know where he's going. Past clothing stores and shoe stores and jewelry stores, past old men sleeping with hanging jaws or otherwise lounging like mannequins on leather chairs, past overflowing kiosks and stand-up signs advertising movies and television newscasters. He stops at windows with sexy items like women's high heeled boots or stores with larger than life images of women touching their moist tongue with a slender finger, and always his impassive face turns sad, his eyelids lower, then close altogether, he grits his teeth, shakes his head twice, moves on. He tries to look nonchalant, worldly, this nine year old boy with the untamed cowlick and the soft glowing skin, his hands in his pockets and his eyes that turned the bat away glancing at this store's name or that store's window display, that young mother's legs or this kiosk's poster selection. But when he gets to an intersection, where narrow side corridors extend in each direction from the main artery that he's traversing, he stops suddenly, peering intently this way and that with squinty eyes, searching for something, it's unclear what, whether the daytime bat or a person, perhaps a guardian, or a playmate, until a series of little dancing steps and a spastic knocking of his knees give away the cause of his apprehension: The boy has to pee. It's clear. He stands there with buried hands, his elbows locked stiff and his shoulders hunched, his knees almost touching and his pigeon-toed feet bouncing, looking for something, some sign, some white outline of a male form on a blue field, some indication of a room that would offer relief to his rapidly filling little boy's bladder, that insolent little organ designed specifically to abuse and embarrass children at the most awkward times.

And then he's off, scuttling down a side corridor, entering stores and canvassing the walls and leaving without the slightest interest in the men's apparel or the CDs or the shiny gems and silver bands. In a ladies clothing store a plump young woman with heavy eyeliner asks if she can help him find anything. Startled, defiant, he hesitates, then squeaks, "My mother." "I'm afraid she isn't here," the young woman says with a smile. "You and I are the only ones in the store." He darts into the corridor, looks both ways, knows that he's lost.

He finds himself gazing into the window of a weird gift store, the displays dark and menacing, the inside strobe unsettling, eerie. He ventures in, his discomfort magically subsiding, his gait slow, deliberate, on his face a look of wonder and slightly concealed fear. Grotesque masks taunt him, sculpted graveyard forms beckon him with bony fingers, gleaming scythes. In the rear, posters of death metal bands with cadaverous female vocalists share black-lighted wall space with voluptuous golden haired pop stars above tables and shelves laden with games and tee shirts, furry handcuffs and kaleidoscopes, incense sticks and fake tattoo appliqués. The place seems a marvel to him and he wanders through it indolently until a thin young woman dressed in black with her waist exposed asks him if she can help him. He's startled by her voice, gapes at her navel a moment and then her cute pale face framed by stringy black hair and shakes his head. "No...No," he says. "I...I'm..." A look of anguish crosses his face and he presses his thighs and knees together and runs past her and out of the store.

I whirl around the four thick cedar columns where they culminate in stainless steel radii at the high ceiling in the center of the mall where I look down at the boy standing at the entrance to a play area filled with romping children sliding and climbing on polyvinyl treats of bacon, eggs, waffles, sliced bananas, and jellied toast, placidly watched over by mothers and an occasional grandmother contented with a respite and adult company, however fleeting. The boy measures himself against a wooden cartoon figure of a happy little freckle faced girl with dark saucer eyes and fat pigtails holding a measuring stick denoting the maximum height allowable for entry. The ruler ends at his brow. He squeezes his eyes shut and his knees bend as spasms pass through his body and he rushes to a bench near some moms and drops onto it, his teeth clamped on a knuckle of his index finger. After a half-minute or so the spasm relaxes and he breathes deeply. I swoop down and enter his troubled head through an ear, take up temporary lodging.

I find no echoes here, no hollowness. I find no joy, either, no jingles from commercials, no repeated refrains from pop songs, no anticipation of Game Boy marathons or pick-up baseball games. What I find instead are banshee cries in a tangled wilderness, strident imprecations, howls, screeching pleas, thudding sensations and thwacks. "You no good son of a bitch," I hear a voice shout, "you little god damned son of a bitch, you should have croaked the minute you were born you no good little son of a bitch you..."

Wisp that I am, I nevertheless find myself churned and tossed about helplessly as this poisonous spew rushes through and around the little cavern that I've come to occupy. "God damn you, you little no good son of a bitch, you fucking worthless little piece of shit." The words clang and clatter like a bin full of steel hubcaps bouncing down a rocky cliff. I rush out the way I entered and zoom upward, seeking skylights and thinner air where only programmed light rock and the ordinary racket of everyday humans can reach me, soothe me.

I fly around, dazed, baffled, surveying the multitude, the dazzling tiled floor, the colorful shop displays, the trees and the ivy and the furnishings. In no time I spot the restrooms down one long corridor, then, a moment later, down a different wing, another. There are men's room and women's rooms, handicapper rooms and unisex rooms, the whole nine yards. The problem is that they're not actually in the corridors. They're located down some blind alleys off the main floor, and the alleys run between stores. If you're looking down the row of storefronts as the boy did, you can easily miss the space between the shops, especially if you're in distress as the boy is. Still, you can ask somebody. There are men walking around in uniforms, black trousers and blinding white shirts with black neckties and broad, round-brimmed black hats with prominent security badges. Earlier I saw the boy avoid them several times—approach, stop in his tracks, turn and hurry away. And, of course, there are the multitudes, but he certainly seems disinclined to ask any of them for help. My hope is that he chose the play area to rest in because of the tendency of little kids to hold their urges until they reach emergency status, at which their mothers have to rush them to the nearest potty. That way the boy could follow them and find his relief.

I don't know if the boy was accompanied by anyone when he came into the mall, but I've seen no one with him. I see everything that's going on, but I'm not omniscient. What I am is, I'm a Wisp. I'm called The Connector. That's my appellation. There are all kinds of Wisps around, but I'm the only one in this mall, and this mall is my domain. My assignment. What I do is, I connect. I connect people with people, people with nature, people with the Earth, people with animals, people with themselves. That's why I'm called The Connector. Of course, in this mall I can only connect people with other people and people with themselves. There's not much nature in here, no Earth or animals. So I work with people. But I can only work with people who are grounded. Whatever that means. Grounded. Well, I know what grounded means, and people who are grounded know what it means, so when I connect with them they respond knowingly and naturally. And often lovingly. It's a good job, connecting. It's all I've ever done.

But this boy isn't grounded. This boy is anything but grounded. This boy is so ungrounded he may as well be an ashtray in a cancer ward. I rush back to the play area, drop down. The boy's face is as tight as stretched plastic wrap, eyes so wide they're nearly rupturing, jaw dropped but lips pursed as though trying to lock up that orifice to prevent some awful outpouring. His tight fists look as if they're gripping a baseball bat but instead they're holding up his chin, which otherwise, by the looks of it, might pulverize his bony clavicle. Then his lids somehow close over those popping eyeballs and his head jerks back and a woman, seated nearby, looks alarmed. I float over her.

"Hey Shelley?" she says, tapping the shoulder of a woman seated next to her but engrossed in a paperback book. "Would you keep an eye on Jason for me for a few minutes? I think that boy over there needs help."

Shelley looks past the woman to the boy. "I'll say he does. I wonder where his mom is. Sure I'll watch him."

The woman rises tall and lean from her bench and strides over to the boy and crouches down. A tear has escaped from under a taut lid on the boy's red face. The woman touches his knee and his lids spring open and he looks down his nose at her. "You look like you need to find a bathroom," she says. "Is your mother around?"

The boy draws back, raises his knees, rests his heels on the bench edge. His eyes betray fear. Finally he shakes his head.

"Come with me," the woman says. He hesitates. "Please," she says. Gently she takes one of his hands and helps him up. A kittenish whimper escapes as he stands. "Do you want to run?" the woman asks, and he shakes his head. "Let's walk then. It's not far."

The boy slips his hand out of his guide's and clenches it. He bobs along beside her, his body contracted, his head aimed down, his eyes focused on the shiny beige tiled floor and the woman's smudged sneakers. The mall din fills his head, competing with the familiar imprecations that, like glowering wraiths, swirl unwanted and despised: "I should stuff those goddamned sheets down your goddamned throat so you croak on your own piss, you no good little son of a bitch you, you *no good* god damned little son of a bitch." Like an endless loop, the chant continues to the beat of strong, bony hands, alternately closed and open, clobbering his doubled up body and the back and sides of his head. He feels the blows as distinctly as he hears the words, but the woman leading him has no idea of this internal catastrophe, this psychic reenactment of the horror he wants to run from. Of course not. How could she? How could anyone? It's enough to know of the physical pain in his midsection, and she's discomfited sufficiently by that. And soon that will be over, it will pass just as fluidly from his memory as the piss itself, and if he remembers anything at all about the ordeal it will be the woman's kindness that elicits a smile, not the blunt heaviness of the near bursting bladder, much less the cacophony of music and curses circling in his head at this moment.

But this is no child of innocence and forgetting. In this head there is no "sacred Yes." No. This is a head destined to foster legions of memories, whole catacombs full of them, stench-filled caverns, subterranean abodes, Stygian furnaces burning innocent children like so many discarded cinders. Yet he demurely accompanies the nice lady, hoping for the moment only that he'll make it on time, that he won't wet his pants, especially out here in this avenue of shops bustling with crowds of kids, or in front of her.

They turn into a corridor of blank concrete block walls and suddenly a door opens and a man almost bumps into them. The boy can see black steel partitions and then white porcelain urinals in the room the man has emerged from, and he begins to rejoice. But the urge to pee now becomes stronger, and he starts a little dance as they recover from the near brush with the man. "Excuse me," the woman says. "This boy's facing an emergency. Can you help us?"

"Sure," the man replies. He holds the door open and follows them in. He gives no sign that he's a bit disconcerted by the woman's cool assertiveness. A toilet flushes and a young man in baggy jeans comes out of a stall, seems alarmed by the presence of the woman in the men's room, utters a baffled profanity. "It's okay, dude," the man tells him. He finishes securing his belt and leaves, repeating his profanity softly. The man leads the boy to a low urinal and says, "Number one or number two?"

"He has to pee," the woman answers. Her voice is loud, almost strident, and the boy looks up at her, startled at her presence, as if he's just noticed it. He takes in her long bent nose for the first time, her tragic motherly eyes. His mouth drops open. He seems paralyzed. He looks as if an anvil had been dropped on his feet.

"You can pee now," the man says.

"It's okay," says the woman. She approaches him. "Please. Hurry."

He looks at her, frozen, then looks at the man. Then at her again. The burn, the burn. His penis feels like the tip of a lit match. His bladder feels ready to burst. Panic begins to enshroud him. "Help him, help him," shouts the woman. "Pull down his pants."

The man approaches and bends down and the boy lets out a series of piercing shrieks, "Aah. Aah. Aaaaah." And then the dam bursts and he's crying and peeing and the man is shouting "Hold it, hold it" as he's fighting with the boy's belt and then the snap on his pant waist and then the zipper. When the pants fall the man rushes behind the boy to avoid the stream shooting out of his little erect penis, he picks the boy up under his armpits and turns, urine rocketing through the tense air like a stream of tracer bullets blasting walls and sinks, even a low mirror, and finally spattering in the urinal, the boy wailing inconsolably as if facing the world's end. Two men enter the room and ask what's happening, and the woman wheels around and instructs them to get a security guard for help. They gawk a moment before rushing out. The boy cries and pees and the man utters reassuring phrases to him, and the woman gazes at the puddle on the floor, the rivulets on the wall. When the torrent weakens and slows to a near stop, and after the last few drops fall to the floor a foot below the boy's dangling feet, the man turns and carries the boy to a stall. He backs into a partly open door and sets the boy down inside and says to wait there, he'll be back soon. The sobbing boy nods, stands there with his hands at his sides, his feet lost in the wet pants around his ankles, the soaked underpants. His sobs are painful to his chest and throat, but he doesn't know how to stop them. He feels that he's alone in an alien world.

The kind man who helped the boy, his dark face and shaved head glistening with sweat, closes the door and rushes past the woman who had led the boy to the restroom, stops abruptly, and turns to her. "I sent a couple of guys who came in here to find security," she tells him. He nods. "I'm going to get the boy some new clothes and be right back. Can you wait for them?" he asks.

"I've got to get back to my child," the woman says. "But I can wait a few more minutes."

"In here? Do you mind?"

"I'm here now. I think I can handle it. If some guys come in and tell me to get out, I'll get out. But I'm a mother, and I'm here now."

"Great. Thanks so much."

"Thank *you.*"

He leaves the room and the woman looks toward the stall and waits. In the stall the boy waits too, his head lowered, his mind exhausted of thought, of image. His eyes catch sight of the roll of tissue paper attached to the black metal wall and he unwinds and tears off a length of it and starts to pat dry his wet legs and scrotum. He tears off several more lengths and when satisfied flushes the paper down the toilet. Again he stands still during the interminable minutes that follow, one loose fist enclosed in his other hand. With nothing else to do and with no forethought he blows a bubble between his lips. As soon as it pops he blows another, then another, this one bigger than the first two, and when it pops the saliva runs down his chin, which he wipes with his palm and fingers. He looks down his nose, purses his lips, blows another and another, thus keeping himself occupied until he hears a knock on the stall door and sees it open. Framed by the steel doorway is a very wide man dressed in black and white like the restroom décor, but with a funny looking flat-brimmed hat with a round crown. "Are you okay, young man?" he asks in a reedy tenor.

The boy looks up at him. Everyone here is so different, he thinks. Not like the people at home, the scary people. The dangerous people. But you never know. This man looks like a balloon he saw on TV during last Christmas season, several stories tall and held by strings, floating along a New York street, except that he's short, shorter than the boy's mother, and he's planted on the floor. But you never know. The boy nods shyly, becomes suddenly alert to his nakedness, looks down at himself and up again, and just sighs.

"What's your name, son?"

The boy hesitates, his eyes dart to the side, up to the man's face, to the side again. "Gabriel," he says feebly.

"Gabriel. Say, like the angel, huh?"

The boy tilts his head, shrugs.

"Is that what everyone calls you?" asks the man.

"No sir."

"Well then, what do they call you, Gabriel?"

A shout heard only by the boy pierces his head. *Gabriel!* He freezes, a frost forms over his hazel eyes. The intonation, loud, edged sharp as a glass shard, explodes in the cavern of his brain with a shattering virulence, each syllable embedding itself like irretrievable shrapnel. *Get in here now, you god damn little son of a bitch you.* Why, why? he wonders. The fulmination resounds ghostly and intense, the hateful words more devastating than mere fists on doubled-up back or open palms on cheeks and ears. *You no good little worthless son of a bitch. You should have croaked the day you were born...* And then, abruptly and without causation, his eyes pop wide and his brain is quiet.

"Gabey," he says triumphantly.

The puffy face smiles. "I have a nephew whose name is Gabey. That's a good name. Well, Gabey, are you here with anyone? Are you here with your mom?"

The boy recoils slightly, engulfs one hand with the other, drops his eyes. "No sir."

"Are you here with anyone else?"

He shakes his head.

"You're alone?"

He simply nods, but his eyes are wide as he looks at the security guard, as if asking his approval to nod. "Excuse me," he hears a voice say, and he sees the man who toted him into the stall. The man nudges the guard, who steps aside.

"How are you doing, my boy?" he asks. "I've got some clothes for you to change into. Here, put these on. We'll wait for you out here." He hands Gabey a pair of jeans and underpants, a pair of socks and a new tee shirt and a belt, all already free of plastic wrappers, pins, and other fasteners. "I think they'll fit you. My own boy is about your age and size." Gabey accepts the folded articles and looks at them humbly as the men close the door and leave him to his privacy.

He sits on the stool to unlace his sneakers, which are mercifully dry, and he slips off his pants and underwear with minimal finger contact and leaves them in a pile. His shirt is wet at the waist, but he doesn't want to touch it for fear of contaminating his head when he pulls it over. Alarm crosses his face as he considers his nakedness and the piss rendered pile at his feet: What if one of his friends would enter and see him like this? Danny. Nate. Larry. What if the neighborhood kids that he liked to beat up whenever they gave him an opportunity saw him? The bloody noses, the gagging pleas, the humiliating tears of those victims, all would be compensated for by this spectacle of the bully bereft—bereft of clothing, of toughness, of family, of home. Besmirched by his own piss, small sobs still escaping now and then, quietly now but betrayed by slightly heaving shoulders and nodding head. He feels beaten up himself, slaughtered by an invisible but merciless foe, a mischievous ghost maybe, a grinning Cheshire cat with multiple legs like a centipede, each ending with a boxing glove-like paw working like pistons to pummel his brain and his spirit.

He heard the flushing of urinals and toilets as he changed, and he heard the running of water and the crushing of paper towels and some whistling, but now as he peeks through a small opening in the stall doorway he sees only the two men, the tall, well built man with the shaved head and a goatee who looks like his hero Barry Bonds and the short, fat man in the black and white costume with the funny hat who, aside from his rounded bulk, seems to blend with the walls, tiles, and stall partitions.

"Well, how do they fit, Gabey? Come on out and let's see," says the Barry Bonds look-alike.

Gabey steps out, leaving the soggy pile on the floor. "You look great," the hero says.

"Bet you feel a lot better too," the fat man adds.

Gabey smiles shyly, and nods.

"Good," his hero says. "Now, did you transfer the stuff from your other pockets into your new jeans?"

The question catches the boy off guard. He rushes back into the stall, but once inside he hesitates to touch the wet pants lying formless on the floor like a puddle. He bends and gingerly picks them up, grimaces as he inserts his hand into a pocket. Slowly he extracts a handkerchief and a wallet, curls his lip, drops the wet cloth but places the wallet into the hand holding the pants. In a flash his free hand attacks and penetrates the other pocket and abruptly stops. His mouth contorted with disgust, he drags something out of the pocket with the paralyzing anticipation of its being something awful, like a liver or a section of a colon. It's a pretzel. Or part of a pretzel. The uneaten half, still a ring, soggy, thick, soiled, inedible. He bought it along with a soda at Aunt Bea's Pretzel and Dog Shop not long after he had entered the mall. He spent a fair amount of time deliberating, studying the menu, peering up and down the mall at other restaurants, pastry shops, and candy stores, before finally deciding on the pretzel. Evidently he ate half of it and planned to munch on the rest as hunger spoke to him. Now he stands there, gazing at it, holding it tightly.

The two men stop talking when they see him standing there. "Whatcha got?" asks the guard. The boy holds up the pretzel half clutched in his right hand, the wallet resting in his left. His innocent face seems to be looking for approval. "Well," the guard says, "I hope you'll wait till the pretzel dries out before you finish it." The dark skinned man glares at his companion, the boy registers surprise at the suggestion, looks down at the pretzel, turns his hand over but doesn't loosen his grip. The dark skinned man bends down, grasps his knees with large hands.

"Hey Gabey, that's quite a wallet you have there. Where'd you get such a cool wallet?"

The boy smiles. "I won it."

"You won it? How?"

"In a pie eating contest."

"A pie eating contest? No kidding. What kind of pie?"

"Blueberry." The boy lets his guard down, shows some enthusiasm. "No handed too."

"No handed? No kidding. You mean you ate a blueberry pie without using your hands?"

"Yeah. We had to keep our hands behind our back. And we were on our knees too."

"On your knees? Really?" The man squats, his arms on his knees, large hands dangling. "On the floor?"

"Yeah." Gabey grins disarmingly. "We were kneeling on the floor with our hands behind our backs, and when the guy blew a whistle we had to bend over down to the floor and eat the pie."

"Was it a whole pie?"

"Yeah. A whole pie. It was in an aluminum tin. We had to stick our faces right in it and eat it. And I won."

"You won."

"Yeah. Boy, was I surprised."

The man laughs. "I'll bet you were a mess." The boy laughs too.

"Yeah I was. I even had that stuff up my nose. In my eyes. Everywhere."

"In your hair?"

"Yeah. Even in my hair."

They laugh and laugh, the rotund guard too, and when the laughter subsides the man who looks like the boy's hero says that he hopes that such a neat wallet was filled with lots of dollars. The boy says Nope and the man says No? "Well, I hope you've got some in there now, don't you."

The boy becomes guarded. He nods. "Because you're going to need it, aren't you," the man says. The boy hesitates, then nods. "How much do you have that you think you'll need?" the man asks. At the boy's silence he says, "Don't worry, my boy. I'm not going to take it. I'm sure you don't even have enough for me to buy myself a good dinner, do you."

"I've got thirty-nine dollars," the boy blurts out.

"Thirty-nine dollars." He slaps his hands together. "Well, that's even more than I'd need for a really good dinner. Thirty-nine dollars. That's really good. That should last a long time, don't you think?"

The boy looks at him, contorts his mouth, tilts his head. He shrugs. The man smiles. "How much did that pretzel set you back?"

"Three dollars and eighty-nine cents. With a soda."

"Three dollars and eighty-nine cents." The man pretends to take some effort at calculations. "Well, that thirty-nine dollars should buy you about ten pretzels and sodas, I'd say. That'll make you a well fed boy for the next week, won't it Gabey."

Self-consciousness, a little fear, some hefty doubt descend on the boy, shut him up in a murky wrap. Just like that. It's as if an animate suit of armor, two sizes too small for him, envelops him, head and all, and without strain closes tightly, leaving neither seam nor bulge. The man sees this immediately, stands and grasps a small shoulder, bends close to him. "I'll be glad to take you home, Gabey," he says.

The shoulder squirms out of his hand as the boy pulls away. He takes two steps back and stops, shaking his head, his eyes fierce. His head shakes and shakes, and then it stops, his eyes defiant and hard. Then it shakes again and stops. He glares at the man's kind face, doesn't move his eyes even as someone enters the room and halts abruptly before bumping into the guard's stout and immovable body. The guard murmurs something to him, the stranger glances from him to the boy to the tall man facing down the boy, nods curtly, turns and leaves the room.

"Gabey?" The man who resembles the boy's hero, the one who bought him fresh new jeans and underpants, leans down, grasps his knees. "Should we call your mother?"

The boy becomes rigid. His eyes widen, his neck tightens, his shoulders contract. I swoop down, enter his ear canal, am battered by a noise reboant of mealtime lion caged and forlorn. The roar bounces on concrete floors, caroms off steel walls and glistening tiles, strikes glass and chrome and hearts and pierces them like a spiked iron shaft. The kind man swims in the boy's sight, a shifting globular image; inside the boy's head fear and despair blow up, shooting their jagged scarring particles furiously outward through a fine gossamer membrane, or an expectant budding universe, the innocence of a child. Words resound too in this clamor, words like rocks tumbling in a steel drum, words like Ya-a-a-h y-a-a-h y-a-a-h, and words like Help help help, silent words in the boy's own little boy's screechy soprano. Then the noise stops and is followed by a curt and quavery yap: "No." He stands still, breathing hard, clutching a damp pretzel and a wallet.

"Gabey." The man's gentle baritone calls as if in the night, a call to a sleepwalking child. The boy still gazes at him, the defiance gone, his head tilted downward. Then his eyes close and a couple of tears slide as far as his cheekbones and drip off his face, dampen the hard, cold floor. "Gabey," the man says.

It's quiet in here now, in this wrecked space, this scarred waste. There's no sound now as he's ushered out the door, the attendant guard holding it open, the kind man's long dark fingers clasping his shoulder. "It'll be all right," the man says, but the promise rings hollow in this head.

I leave that sad place, fly out, up into the bland cheerfulness of commercial amusement, the vapid world of desire and dreams. Far below me walk a tall, nicely dressed man and a boy, they're holding hands, in the boy's free hand is half a pretzel, he walks with his head down. They walk slowly toward an exit to the outside world, where I wish I could be with the boy, where I wish I could hold him, envelop him like a garment, or like the folded wings of a bat, wings that stretch and wrap and protect. I can't do that, though. I'm a Wisp, but I'm assigned to this mall, this vast, vapid space, to connect with people who are grounded. Whatever that means. Like that kind man who's walking with him.

I hope that man is a bat.

GANGSTER

The sun is September bright, the shadows of the brick school building and the flagpole crisp and hard edged. The small kids are orderly as they parade behind two adults down the path from their exit to the sidewalk; they're careful to not step on the sharp yellow grass, as if on orders, and they walk smartly, briskly. They're cute in their colorful beginning of the year duds and their little backpacks, and they pass without hesitation the two older boys standing on the sidewalk; some of them even chirp a greeting like fragile songbirds, and they continue until they reach a bus stop halfway down the block. The older kids follow in order and the boys among them, seeing the suspicious strangers, cluster together and as they pass they cast wary sidelong glances at them. Some follow the younger kids and some go the other way. Some engage in group small talk, but not close to the strangers. A few stragglers leave the building separately.

"Let's get this next kid," Jesse says, nodding his head sideways toward a pudgy boy with a stubbled head walking alone. "Fucking marine."

They approach him, hands in pockets.

"Hey," says Chris. "Lend me a buck."

The boy stops. He dips his head a bit, thickens his neck, frowns. He's taller than Jesse, whom he seems to recognize as he twitches his brow and widens his eyes, but he has to look up to meet those of Chris. As soon as he catches sight of them, their coldness, he drops his head again, shifts his gaze back at Jesse.

"I ain't got a buck," he says.

Jesse looks up to Chris and his mouth contorts into an ugly sneer. He returns to the boy, whose head is tilted, eyes directed away, to the side.

"He says he wants a fucking dollar. Give him a fucking dollar."

The boy looks from Jesse to Chris and sees his scowl, too hard for a twelve year old, and hears his breathing. He dips his eyelids, his mouth twitches slightly, his shoulders sag almost imperceptibly, but Chris picks up on it and spits. The boy's right hand reaches into a pocket and fumbles in there and then it slips back out. He holds a wadded up dollar in his open palm and Chris snatches it.

"The rest too," he orders. His voice is still pre-adolescent but it's husky and dim and flat, tough to a younger kid.

"That's all I got," the boy protests.

Jesse extracts a knife from his pocket but doesn't switch open its six inch blade. The boy's eyes move toward it and then jump to Chris's face, as if seeking his protection. Chris stares silently at him. In an instant the boy's hand disappears into his pocket again and reappears with two bills folded into small tight squares which Chris takes with a mocking delicacy.

"Good boy." He pats a round pink cheek, rubs the stubbled head. "See you tomorrow."

They turn and walk away and the boy stands there like a pathetic carved toy. A couple of other kids slowly approach him, but no one calls an adult. Chris and Jesse walk on and cross the street, where they're joined by two others. "We hit the jackpot," says one of them, Ronnie, whose voice is changing. "Six and a half bucks. Two kids."

"And we got, what? Three," adds Jesse.

"That's a start," Chris says.

They walk in the streets of their neighborhood past its neat frame houses from the Depression era, with their screened in porches and painted shutters shaded by blue spruces and oaks. At the edge of their turf they enter a small shopping district and buy sodas at one of the small diners, then tramp through a nearby weedlot approaching a steep railroad bed. At the foot of the overgrown bed, hidden beneath scrub brush and sumacs, is a depression several feet deep that looks like a mass grave abandoned before any internment. Blackened two by ten planks, four to six feet long, lie on narrow ledges shaped by the hands and haunches of more than one generation of the disaffected and the wandering. Jesse raises a plank and finds a couple of magazines. "Hey, a new one," he squeals. He holds one up to show the others the cover photo of a woman squeezing her oversized breasts. Ronnie snatches it from him, takes a seat and opens it, leaving Jesse with the older one. Chris passes around cigarettes and they smoke. Jesse looks up from his magazine.

"You see that kid's face when I pulled the knife?" he asks Chris.

"You had to pull a knife?" Ronnie says. "He giving you trouble?"

"Nah. I just thought I'd let him see it. I didn't open it. But did you see his face?"

"He was scared shitless," said Chris. He was playing with a leaf, folding it, running his nail along its veins. His cigarette was dangling from his lips and the smoke was bothering his eyes, so he dropped the butt on the dirt and stamped it out. "The look of fear all over his face. Nice to have power, ain't it."

"Damn straight," Jesse says, pleased with himself. He pulls out the knife, swishes it open, tests the blade, admires it.

"That could make quite a slice, couldn't it," the fourth boy, Mickey, observes.

"A slice?" Jesse slashes the air. Then he penetrates it with a thrust. "A fucking puncture."

"A puncture!" Ronnie laughs.

"This blade would've let the air out of that fat little prick back there just like in a fucking cartoon."

Chris's face changes, his eyes glare. The pudgy boy's face materializes before them, the fear that tightened up his facial muscles, the slight twitching of his mouth, the almost imperceptible slumping of his shoulders, the subtle twinge in his eyebrow that bespoke submission, the deflation of spirit, the sag of defeat.

"When we gonna use the blade for something serious?" asks Ronnie.

"We got plenty of time, man. No hurry," Chris says.

THE...COAT (AND CAP)

Everything had been just dandy two hours ago for Ambrose George. He had been sitting on his favorite bench under great theatrical elms in the park, early evening, skaters rolling past, joggers, walkers, quiet humble dogs, squirrels, the whole teeming shebang. The golden September light was his favorite; there was a comfort to it, an invitation to indolence, a delicious slackness in its vast smiling resplendence. Knowing that the hard–edged shadows of trees and towering buildings would swallow up this precious luminosity in no time, he sprawled on the bench, a split-open marionette, inviting the sun to fill him with rays of sweet repose, of peace, of something maybe transcendent, something miraculous, something to get him through another night alive and sane.

They, the nights, had been getting pretty scary lately, his existence pretty precarious, tenuous even. Why, just last night he ran into a the driver's door of a taxi, its rear view mirror jamming his ribs hard, thank God they're rounded and plastic nowadays he thought later, the cabbie's brown face aghast. The taxi had just started to move forward after the light turned green but Ambrose, for some reason suddenly and inexplicably confused, darted off the curb, crossed one lane and ran smack into it. Oddly enough, he knew with the first step that he shouldn't be crossing, but he felt compelled to do it, unable to stop even when the cabbie's startled double-take registered with split second swiftness in his mind. So he ran into the car, got jabbed by the mirror, bounced off and spun away back toward the curb, caught himself embracing a trash container. Good thing no traffic was coming in the curb lane, he thought. I would've been dead for sure. Good thing, too, his ribs weren't broken, though they still hurt, and it hurt like hell when he coughed. Well that's okay, he thought. There were plenty of times he'd felt worse that that.

Let's see, that was last night, he recalled. It's been like that every night lately, or at least it seems so. One thing or another. He lit a cigarette, inhaled deeply, and spread his arms out on the back of the bench. His mouth open wide, he let the smoke escape slowly, enjoying its mild disorder in the weak breeze and its gradual dissipation. Ah, he thought. Look at all these beautiful people. Two women hurried by in animated conversation, one in slacks, the other in an above the knee skirt, both in spiked heels. Following them a strutting man with a leashed shar-pei. The mall was busy now. Boys on skateboards doing tricks, old couples, tourists with bobble heads, lovers. The whole usual bunch, they might be the same people he saw every time he sat here. Backlit against sloping green lawns past the trees, accompanied by the perpetual hum of distant traffic, the gaiety of thrush songs, the energy of hip hop. Skaters to his right, down by the bandshell. A graceful, muscular, bare-chested man gliding with a bottle on his head. Beautiful. He smoked the cigarette down, tweaked off the lit ash, placed the filter in his shirt pocket.

Two nights ago, was it? He'd puked over a low railing onto a narrow lawn at the foot of an Indian restaurant down on Sixth Street. God, what was he doing there? Gagging and coughing, and then vomiting, all so suddenly. And then the stuff came again, ten steps away, between two parked cars, people walking by. He stepped off the curb and slid in it, a perfect cartoon fall, one foot leading the other into the air, the torso following and flattening out, the breathless descent flat onto his back. He felt his head dribble twice and thought, "This is it. It's all over." He thought, "I'm lying in my vomit." His eyes searched for a sympathetic face, someone to ask if he was all right. He felt no pain, and that scared him. He moved an arm, then a leg, he turned his head from side to side. "Hell, might as well get up," he said to himself. "You okay, guy?" he heard someone ask as he struggled up. Nice guy, big bushy eyebrows.

His shoulder still ached but that was all. No other pain, no headache, no dizziness, nothing. Ambrose George closed his eyes and smiled. "Close calls, close calls," he thought. "I'm damn lucky to be alive."

Splayed and limp as he was, that was as critical as Ambrose George's thinking got. He had given up trying to figure out how or why he got down onto Sixth Street, why his gag reflex was so hyperactive, why he would find himself vomiting unexpectedly into flower beds and hedgerows. He didn't like any of that shit, but he was alive, wasn't he? And wasn't that all that mattered?

Ambrose George felt peaceful, and that was only two hours ago. Two hours ago, and seemingly in another city. He felt he could sleep there on that bench, late sunlight resting on him like a blanket, rhythmic footsteps drumming past. But as the wafting breeze of sleep began to transport him, a muted whimpering sound made him open his eyes and swing them to the right, where he saw a young woman with long straight hair and rimless glasses shaking her head and waving her right hand palm down. A young man, very tall and lean, gestured an "It's okay" with both hands as he approached Ambrose.

"Excuse me," he said with a tone of genuine deference. "We're looking for Strawberry Fields. Can you tell us where to find it?"

Ambrose took a moment to smile before answering, to bathe in the warmth of a stranger's voice directed at him, for a change, without vituperation or sarcasm—indeed, with a younger person's appropriate courtesy. He looked the couple over, the young man's sandy hair, curly and neat, his winning features, naïve, eager eyes, unbuttoned shirt, the young woman's pinched nostrils and thick lips, her bulging breasts fighting against the tight confinement of her bright blue halter, her cute little pierced navel. Not bothering to see if his ravenous gaze made her self-conscious, his eyes returned to her partner. "Sure," he said. "Gladly."

For a moment Ambrose George sat frozen, then, unexpectedly, he sprang into motion, his outstretched arms flying from the bench and enfolding his chest and his spread legs drawing together with one whipping across the other knee, the fabric covering his crossed leg riding halfway up his calf to expose several bruises mottling his ankle bone and his sharp-edged shin. He was hunched now, appearing to be lost in thought, an oily lock of brown hair reaching down his forehead to his eye. At what she must have thought a comic sight, the young woman's hand jerked up to her mouth to muffle a gasp of surprise and a titter, her eyes bulging with glee, while her companion threw back his head and shook it as if in disbelief. Ambrose pointed.

"You go over there where they're skating and you take a left," he said. "You walk a little way and you come to a Y and you take a left." He stopped, tilted his head, cradled his chin between thumb and index finger. "No, you turn right. You turn right." He nodded. "You turn right, then, then you keep walking..." He looked confused, he cut himself off again. He sprang from his seat.

"Look," he said, "let me take you there. I've got to get going anyway." The young woman flashed a wary look at her companion, but he shook it off. "It's just a little walk, but my feet know the way better than my head. Follow me now. Okay?"

He walked fast, gaining steps on them, whirling about to see if they were near. "It's a beautiful place," he said, his monologue like raspy bird chatter. "Lots of people still make the pilgrimage. Wonderful place. I sit there a lot myself." He almost danced along the walks, jumping like a child off the path onto the grass and back again, spinning and babbling and coughing, occasionally jerking downward and holding his ribcage, while the young strangers followed wordlessly. Here he was, Ambrose George, late of rendezvous with taxi doors and his own puke, escorting two children to a garden of butterflies and splendor and deep meaning, fluttering along the paths and through clusters of pedestrians like a buzzed major domo. And that was only a couple of hours ago, while the early evening sunlight still filtered through the trees of the park and the looming buildings along its western border.

And then they were there, Ambrose George bowing low and sweeping his hand through the air over the flat memorial to the fallen idol who took his own ghosts with him, the words Strawberry Fields greeting them amid long stemmed roses, folded notes, a few trinkets, and a used tissue.

For a moment he watched the mute young couple approach slowly and stand with a few other observers amid the usual pedestrian traffic, listened to the sounds—the cars, the buses, the horns, the loud vulgarities of street men under the nearby arbor. He turned, spotted a particular bench that was unoccupied, a look of childish delight lit up his face as he quickly walked to it. Before sitting down he bent forward, grimacing as he grabbed his rib cage, and read the inscription on the brass plaque attached to it. It was his favorite piece of writing, literature for the ages: simple, fascinating. THE WOOL LOVES SANDY SUE, it said. He smiled broadly. The Wool loves Sandy Sue. "Hah! Amazing!" he said aloud as he seated himself.

His smile faded and the hollows returned to his cheeks, but his face looked serene. Yes indeed, he thought. The Wool still loves Sandy Sue. He extracted a handkerchief from his pocket and rubbed it across the plaque. The Wool has loved Sandy Sue a long time. The Wool will keep on loving Sandy Sue for a long time. He nodded. "Ahh," he said aloud; and he thought, I wish I was The Wool.

He looked up and his eyes sought the young couple he had guided over here. Not spotting them at the memorial, he surveyed the lines of benches, none of which was occupied by anyone interesting looking and few by anyone younger than forty or so. He looked along the walks and paths, off the pavement to the thickets and yards. They were gone. Ambrose George felt something vacate him. It wasn't a sudden emptying, an outpouring, but it didn't sneak out either, it didn't ooze or seep, it just went, an unquantifiable bit at a time, and he felt it leave. God he wanted them to be there, the young couple. He wanted to see them there, holding hands, gazing solemnly down at the Strawberry Fields marker, reading the word "Imagine," mingling their gratitude to him for bringing them to this hallowed segment of the city with their respect and love for the fallen hero honored and celebrated with roses and notes and trinkets. At very least he wanted them to say something more to him, like maybe "Hey, thanks, guy, for bringing us here." Something civil like that.

He felt himself going numb. "Oh shit," he thought. He had one more cigarette, which he found in his shirt pocket, he lit it, his fingers holding the match with preternatural calmness as though they didn't belong to him, they separated and the match dropped between his knees to the ground. He inhaled softly and removed the cigarette from his mouth with his thumb and index finger and let his hand fall to his thigh, where his fingers held the little smoking cylinder until they sensed the heat of the lit end and released it to join the match on the pavement. His eyes rested on the word "Imagine."

From some nether region came the command to rock his head and he complied, slowly, almost imperceptibly, as if comforting himself. "Imagine." To imagine takes an act of will, or maybe an impulse. No such thing as an act of will was possible for Ambrose George now, and the only impulse he could experience was to gently, absently, rock his head. But the images that filled his head appeared without effort. They were just there, these images, assailing him as they so often did without provocation or plan, without mercy. Florie's smooth face, fine, fine hairs on her cheeks, the sharp edges of her toenails, paper, written words, wavy auburn hair, stairways, swirling trees, all these images, her sweet alto voice, her favorite song, "*...ribbons, scarlet ribbons, scarlet ribbons for her hair...*"

And then her head bouncing down a street. His broken first car, her broken high school body. His swollen hands. Bloody hands. Torn open on coarse tree bark, brick walls, the unforgiving steel of car doors. And the ghosts. Everywhere. Hallway wraiths. Schoolyard wraiths. Wraiths in bars, in bottles, under car hoods, hiding in pant legs. Wails. Sirens. And always Florie's soft voice and her song, "*...scarlet ribbons, for her hair.*"

You get to be fifty-two and you think you've earned the right to forget that you killed your sweetheart, you lived and she didn't, you walked away whole and she was scooped up, you think the dues you've paid in your lonely survival should ease your bond, get you through the old grief. But it doesn't happen that way. No, the noises become louder, the images more vivid, and both more frequent, more persistent, habitual even. As if the Vicodin and bourbon fix in your little apartment isn't enough; you can't go down to the park and take a little walk and sit down on a bench and walk a half mile from one place to another without another one.

Time went by and Ambrose George stopped rocking his head and looked up. Dusky light, the strange smell of charcoal, the benches full of people, mostly men, some animatedly talking, people standing around the circle on the ground. "You like a smoke?" The voice was nearby. Ambrose's head slowly turned to his right. A man, a little older than he, with thick white hair and a heavy mustache, smiled at him.

"Sure would," said Ambrose, weak, spent, but relieved to be distracted. "Love one."

The man shook an L&M out of his nearly full pack and lit it, then gave it to Ambrose, who closed his eyes and inhaled deeply, threw back his head with the cigarette held greedily between his pursed lips. "Mmm thanks," he said.

"Think nothing of it," the voice, reedy, friendly, returned. Then, after a pause, "You were in another universe, my friend."

Ambrose winced, breathed in more smoke. He shut tight his eyes and, as if in pain, lowered and turned his head, finally exhaled. "I guess so."

"I hope the visit was a happy one."

"Huh!" His mouth played with the cigarette. He opened his eyes and rolled them to the right corners and took measure of the man. Oh shit, he thought. He's going to preach.

"You know," the man said, stretching out his legs and crossing his ankles, but looking straight at Ambrose, "I used to have those troubled reveries, too. Deep ones, dark ones." Abruptly he sat upright, legs drawn in. "Then one day Jesus visited me."

• • • •

"Where is that fucking thing?" The question screams in his mind as he runs. He never ran so fast before, or so far. Without stop. More than a dash, he sprints, tearing down streets and alleys, whizzing along sidewalks and parkways, dodging trees and hydrants and people like a whitetail doe. "Where is it? Jesus, where is it? I've got to find that fucking thing." His face is panicked, his movements, particularly when he has to skid to a stop at an intersection or a crawling disposal truck blocking an alleyway, antic, all flailing arms and stuttering steps in his worn and soiled oxfords. He runs into a barricade crossing Broadway by 180th Street, picks himself up with a series of mighty curses and resumes running, a fresh tear in his pants, skinned palms bleeding, his rib cage roaring with pain and he runs. Over sand and gravel where pavement had lain he races the buses, the taxis, colors and lights ablur, he runs as if to save his life, or else to catch eternity, he turns onto some narrow street and runs to its end two blocks away and turns left and runs down the street deserted save for guano flecked automobiles heavy breath and rapid footfalls like skipping stones. "Where is it, where is it? I've got to find that fucking thing," he shouts aloud.

He's looking for his fucking coat, is what he was looking for. It's a topcoat, black, wool, limper than when he had bought it some years before but still not bad, he thought he looked good in it yet, he felt a little gentlemanly in it, in fact, it made him proud, he stood just a little straighter when he wore it. But somehow, some time between last night or the night before and this evening, he lost it, he thinks it was somewhere around this area, Washington Heights, his home turf, where else could it be? It was some time between his fall in his vomit two nights earlier and now, he is sure of that, because he had worn it that night, he thinks, though he couldn't be positive after all because all he knows without question is that he couldn't find it at home when he stopped there for a a few more Vicodin after leaving the Strawberry Fields preacher and he needs to have it, and all he's concerned with now is not running into trees or cars or being hit by them or attacked by dogs.

He's running up a hill beginning to pant hard past restaurants and Camel signs and markets, red and blue and yellow lights, he sees the luminosity of towers ahead, the George Washington Bridge. Not there, he hears a voice in his head advise. Turn around, it's down some side street, it's not there. He darts off the sidewalk and only then thinks to look for traffic, his body dodges nimbly an oncoming motorcycle, his consciousness, such as it is, having nothing to do with the move, it's his body alone that saves itself. Like a driverless runabout over endless smooth water he runs, his breath like a chugging motor on an open sea, and then he finds himself at the edge of the world and he stops, teeters, catches himself. Only it isn't the edge of the world, it isn't the depthless precipice his eyes at first led him to think it was, it's a stairway, a long concrete descent into another part of his world many stories below. He knows this staircase, he knows the city below, it's a teeming place, he loves it, but right now all he knows is that his fucking coat is down there somewhere, and so he starts his descent, wasting no time he takes the steps two at a time and when there's a landing he jumps down three or four of them. Halfway down his heel catches the edge of a step and he flies and falls as he did in his vomit a couple of nights earlier, this time his tailbone hits first and a paralyzing pain surges through his head and out his gaping mouth in a sound and a curse so vile and pathetic as to nearly drown out traffic in the streets below and televised announcers in the apartments above. He writhes slowly on the steps in wormlike contortions and whimpers and calls upon some god over and over, and finally he hears a voice ask him if he's all right. It's a woman's voice; he opens his eyes and focuses them on her equine teeth and shiny black hair and he shakes his head. "Oh god, no," he says, almost crying.

She leans over, hands on her denim knees. "Can I do anything?" she asks earnestly. "Shall I call 911?"

Ambrose George groans an impressive groan. "Oh god no," he says again. "Please, can you just help me up?"

The woman extends a slender hand to him and he, flailing, latches onto it. At the same time as he begins to lift his back he feeels something enclose his upper body and he sees another person, a dark and glistening young man, helping the woman by lifting him from the steps. Eventually they stand together, Ambrose's grimaces and moans speaking for him, the young man holding him steady, the woman withdrawing.

"Sure I can't call 911?" she asks.

"I'll be okay," he answers. "Really. I'm looking for something."

"Whatcha looking for, man?" the man asks.

"I'm looking for my fucking coat,"Ambrose answers, his voice quite thin. "You seen it?"

The man looks at the woman, then back at Ambroase. "Hey, I'm afraid I haven't seen your fucking coat, man. What's it look like?"

"Long. Black. Wool." He grimaces, takes in a deep breath between clenched teeth, holds his lower back with both hands.

"Hey," the man says, "I'll keep my eyes open for it, okay?"

"Appreciate it." Ambrose tries to smile.

"You take care now, okay?"

Ambrose nods, his mouth drawn and lips separated, teeth tightly clenched. The man skips down the steps and the woman resumes her climb, and Ambrose looks out over the city. He feels a cool mist surround him which soon, as he hobbles downward holding his back and grimacing, turns into a drizzle. Down, down he goes, like an awkward marionette given life by a jokester, two things on his mind: his pain and his fucking coat. The one, it seems, a mere means to the procurement of the other. And when he has the other, what then? Then he puts it on, that's all, he puts it on and warms up in it, he's getting chilled now in the fine rain, he looks down at the slick pavement glaring in the street light and he shivers a bit, nothing the fucking coat wouldn't remedy.

Finally his worn oxford touches sidewalk and with a moan he begins running again, not so fast this time, in fact his motion is more a laborious shamble at first than a run but after a block he's picked up the pace and after two blocks, with Broadway just ahead, he's almost in full stride.

When he gets to Broadway he sets off to cross it but finds his way blocked by a yellow plastic netlike barricade that keeps him in the middle of the street. He turns to run alongside the barricade and spots an approaching bus, he skids to a stop and turns as the bus pulls alongside in its narrow lane and he feels the steel of its side brush and rub against his arm, he's squeezed between the bus and the net fence but the fence gives and the bus moves on and he starts running again, following that bus as if it were his guide. Suddenly there's traffic on both sides of him, the work area's behind him and all four lanes are open with Ambrose George in the center bedazzled by headlights and car horns. He swerves to his right and hears the muted screech of tires on the wet pavement and he feels a bump, he hops and spins and lands, signals to the frightened driver that he's okay, he lowers his head and leans forward to start himself off again and hears more horns, he looks up and his body dodges another skidding car and then he finishes crossing and runs another block until he collapses onto a bench, doubled over, his breath squealing like train brakes. He feels a weight on his shoulder but he can't acknowledge it.

Ambrose George hawks up a wad of thick mucous and spits it out and looks at the hand still resting on his shoulder. He sits up and sees a heavy man leaning over the back of the bench, shoulders wide enough to skateboard on, face intense and stern, eyebrows precipitously arched. He slumps, tries to ignore the intruder, lowers his head, strains of "Scarlet Ribbons" weave through his brain, he sees images of Florie's bright teeth, wide pores on tanned legs, a shiny knee, closed casket. *Scarlet ribbons, for her hair.* All these years of silent woe. Gnawing away his feelings, his spirit, like rats a wasted and forgotten prisoner. Too late. It's too late now. He shakes his head. God, it gets tiring, he thinks.

His hands, torn from his earlier fall, lie open, palms up, on his lap. Despite the medication he swallowed on his brief stop home between the park and this corner bench, his stiffening lower back fills his entire body with a crackling pain. He's still breathing hard but rhythmically now, and he feels the weight of both the man's meaty hands on his shoulders, just resting there.

"Are you okay, my friend?" The man's voice is a gentle, smooth bass. "Can I give you a hand?"

Ambrose George hesitates to acknowledge the invitation. His immediate wish is to be lifted into the arms of the big man and be whisked away to some snug bower of safety and consolation, redolent of thyme and rosemary. But after summoning up and spitting out another lump of phlegm, he merely shakes his head again.

"I'm fine," he says in a weak croak, then clears his throat. "I'm okay."

"You look like you're in need, my friend," the man gently persists. "Perhaps I can help."

Oh no, Ambrose thinks. Not Jesus again. Christ, he'd been trying to get that other guy's piety out of his mind for the last two hours, one of the reasons he stopped at home. Vicodin and bourbon were supposed to help with that.

"I'm just trying to find my fucking coat," he says. "That's all."

Suddenly he's aware of his soaked hair, the heavy shirt clinging to his skin, the saturated seat of his pants from the bench he's sitting on. "Can you help me find my fucking coat? That's all I need."

"You look like you need more than that, friend."

Ambrose rotates his head to peer at the man, his torso rotates too and he grimaces and lets out a groan. "Jesus," he says. "I wrecked the hell out of my back." He fastens onto the man's broad, severe face, sees that his eyes are kind. "And what kind of help do you suppose I need?"

"I think I know," says the man. "Do you know?"

"Yeah, I know what I need." Ambrose George grins like a dying badger. "I need my fucking coat, that's what I need. You know where my fucking coat is at?"

The heavy man stares at him like a pitiless judge, but Ambrose doesn't shrink. "I think I may know that too," he says. Ambrose's eyes widen. The man's face remains stern but his voice softens, the pace of his words slows. "I heard of someone chortling over a coat he found. It's a topcoat?" Ambrose nods. "Wool? Black? Well worn?" To each of these descriptions Ambrose utters a joyful "Yep, yep." The man smiles and his brow finally smooths out.

"He's in an alley just two blocks from here." The man raises a hand from Ambrose's shoulder and points east. "Just two blocks. Turn left and you'll see the alley. I think you'll find him down there."

The man rushes his enormous bulk around the bench and helps as Ambrose struggles to stand. "Thanks," Ambrose says through clenched teeth, his torn hands working to mold his back into something resembling uprightness. "That's all I want. Just my coat.

I need that fucking coat."

"You'll soon have it, my friend." The huge man smiles and without signal embraces Ambrose like a corpulent cloud. When he releases him, he deftly withdraws his wallet and extracts a business card. "Call me if you need some help. I'll be right over, wherever you are."

Ambrose puts the card in his pocket without glancing at it. He nods. "Gotta get my coat," he says.

For the first time since he escorted the young lovers to Strawberry Fields a couple of hours ago, Ambrose George walks toward a destination. The drizzle had stopped and he's feeling chilled, his pace is slow and agonizingly labored, he knows this neighborhood but hadn't thought to search it, for some reason he stayed west of Broadway. He wonders about the card he was handed, what does it say? what kind of outfit does this guy run? what kind of church is he selling? Christ, I don't need that shit. Never helped a bit. None of it. Church never helped. Fucking never helped. Well, not for long anyway. Work, fuck work. Never helped. Reading. People. Whistling. None of it. None of it works. None of them takes away the shit. You put on the nice clothes and you wear them for a while and then eventually you got to take them off. They wear out or they stink. Or they get ugly. Don't mean nothing no more. At the entrance to the alley he stops, tries to straighten his back, his hands are throbbing, he takes a deep breath. "Damn," he mutters and clutches his ribs. "Fucking coat."

He shuffles down the alley hearing only a squish from his oxfords and occasional drops of water fallen from tree leaves shimmying in the occasional breeze. He coughs up phlegm and spits it out, hears it land. After a few more steps he halts at a grumbling sound, then a loud hawk and another sound, a ptooey. He looks around: fences and dumpsters, patches of grass visible from gay window lights, looming squared off structures black against gray sky, backlit by invisible street lamps. Distant accordion and brass music, sounds of Mexico, joyous in the night. Then a voice. "Hey!" Ambrose George forgets his bruised body, looks all around, heart pounding. The voice could have come from anywhere, could have issued from the damp night itself, could have been directed at anyone.

"Hey! You lookin' for your fucking coat?" The voice resounds in the alley, a pure and rich baritone, but challenging, menacing.

Ambrose is only too glad to answer. "Yeah. Where are you?"

"Over here, smart-ass."

Ambrose scours the darkness, trains his eyes on the back of a building to his right. "Where the hell is over here smart-ass?"

"You are a smart-ass, aren't you," replies the voice. "You want your fucking coat and you act like a smart-ass. If you want your fuckin' coat, you ought to be a bit more fucking civil."

"You're over there, aren't you?"

A thick beam of light appears, a flashlight beam. It aims straight upward, then suddenly horizontal, upward again, horizontal again the opposite way, then at Ambrose, in his eyes as if drawn to them, but for only an instant before it jerks back to the wall of the building from where it seems to have originated. Ambrose sees a shadow move against the illuminated wall of the building, he sees a wooden porch extending across the width of the building on what appears to be the second story. The speaker with the beautiful baritone is on a rotten sofa-bed on top of a huge closed dumpster. From the back of the sofa the figure could climb over the porch railing.

"Yeah, over here. I've got your fuckin' coat, and I'll tell you one thing. It's kept me plenty warm."

"I know," Ambrose yells back. "It's a plenty warm coat."

"Yeah. But it stinks like fuckin' puke."

"Yeah? I never noticed."

"You never noticed. Jesus, it's foul as fermented pig shit."

"Can I have it back?"

"I don't know if you can have it back. Fuckin' coat anyway."

"Hey man, just let me have it back, huh? I need that fucking coat."

"You need this fucking coat? You need this fuckin' coat? Well I'll tell you what. You can have this fuckin' coat. But I get to keep the bottle."

Ambrose freezes. That's right, he thought. That's right. I left a bottle in there. "You can have the bottle."

"Not much more in it anyway. Damn good vodka." He raises his voice. "Like I say, the fuckin' coat's been keeping me nice and warm."

"I'm glad of that. I'm plenty cold right now."

The coat swoops down on him and he half blocks, half catches it, stands there with it in his arms. It's heavy and damp, smells bad. "Go on, put it on," the voice says. "Warm up. It's good for that, if you can stand the stench."

Ambrose hesitates a moment, curls his mouth at the odor, it's like dead vermin in a wall. Then he obeys, clenching his teeth as he tries to get his second arm into a sleeve. When it's on he shrugs his shoulders, turns to walk away, stops and throws out a word of thanks and resumes a slow pace.

"Hey, wait a minute."

He freezes, his heart races, anticipating trouble.

"Here."

He turns around, sees something whirling toward him, it lands on the ground nearby, he approaches the object, stands there as if inspecting it, he slowly lowers himself to a crouch but loses his balance and falls, cries out and lands on his knees and hands. He reaches for the thing and picks it up. The flashlight beam lands on it and he sees that it's a green cap with the letters VT on the crown. The stiff curved visor is a bit creased, but Ambrose is thrilled. "My cap," he shouts. "God damn! You found my fucking cap. Holy Christ almighty. My cap!"

"Ah, it's the little things, ain't it," says the voice.

"This is a big thing, believe me. I love this cap."

"Go in peace, smart ass."

Ambrose chuckles, puts it on and pumps his clenched hands and turns. He walks a little faster now that the cap is on his head, but he gets only a half dozen steps before the baritone splits the air once again.

"Hey Ambrose. Hey. Ambro-o-o-sia. Yo, Fuckhead."

"Huh?" He stops abruptly, turns back. "How do you know my name, man?"

"Come here, a little closer. Here's something else."

Again a dark thing flies toward him, lands ten feet in front of him. As he approaches it, the beam of light reveals another garment. He slowly squats, holds his balance this time, lifts a jacket, it feels wool, it's a faded plaid, his face brightens again. "It's my sport jacket." He looks up, tries to see a face, is blinded by the light. "Where'd you get this?" he shouts. "I didn't even know I lost it."

The beam suddenly disappears. "Ha haaa, ha haaa," laughs the voice. "Ha haaa."

Ambrose George approaches the big street slowly. He's fighting off tears, he doesn't know why, a snuffle arises and escapes, he spits phlegm and covers his lower face with his bunched up sport coat. The big street is bright with overhead lamps and reflections from the wet pavement, and it's noisy with traffic, buses puffing diesel fumes and taxis plying the wet asphalt, swerving to avoid barricades, enormous semis with fruit laden cornucopias painted on the trailers, growling city trucks reeking of garbage. Around him everywhere life walks on and slides and swirls, surges and charges. It drives by and honks and squawks and roars, it trundles and skips and spurts, saunters and dashes. On the fringe of city electric and denizens vibrant, Ambrose George stands there hunched at 185th and Broadway in his fucking coat and Vermont cap hands holding his damp wool sport coat to his face, a garment that doesn't stink like rotting vermin, and his mind drifts to the card in his pocket. Maybe he'll look at it. Read it. Call the guy.

Maybe he'll do that.

THE HOLY BURROW

Behind his house where two garages faced two others at the place where the alley stopped mid-block, Chris hid out in brush thick and high enough to hide a crouching adolescent who could peer out at neighbors in their yards or strangers on the more distant sidewalk but who would not be seen by them if he sat still. Even if he moved he would not be seen by them unless on a windless afternoon or evening after supper they saw the branches tremble and the leaves shiver and they ventured to take a closer look.

Chris spent a lot of hours per week in those low weedy bushes, unplanted and untended, and in the present springtime barren, unflowered. Sometimes he even crouched there unseen, immobile, like a boyish Buddha with a cowlick, host to spiders and ants, friend of twigs and hard soil, while neighborhood boys played basketball in the pocked and cracked apron of the farthest garage and he watched them through tiny openings among the leaves as through a *camera oscura*, breathing in the bright colors of tee shirts and shorts, tasting the beads of sweat and the slapping hands, listening to the dazzling and chaotic patterns, the dizzying architecture of movement like a skyline during an earthquake.

Chris shifted, prepared to rise, to go to his home and face the music. He owned no timepiece but he knew that supper was served and perhaps already cold and he knew there'd be hell to pay to his mother for being late. He was scared and he had no good excuse to offer for his tardiness other than the truth, and he couldn't tell her that. How could he? How could he tell her that on this day of days, this the last day of his thirteenth year, his tongue had tasted an earlobe for the first time? No, how could he tell her that his fingers had thrummed soft little toes, felt the fine sharp edges of nails not his own? No, no…and how could he tell her that, most amazing of all, most unforgettably and magically—indeed, how could he tell her?—he was late because in the basement rec room of Karen's little house his fingertip had for the first time circumscribed something swollen and firm under a soft cotton shirt, something alive and surprisingly pointed and hard as a ginger snap, something his finger could see because his eyes weren't permitted access despite his pathetic eager puppydog face and his cherubic smile.

"Hey Chris," Karen had intoned, her hands sifting his hair. "Chris." Her voice was soft but commanding. "Hey Christian."

"Huh?" he breathed. His hand went to her face, traced her jawline.

"You're really some Christian, Mister Christian."

"I am? What're you talking about?"

"You know, you're leading me right into sin, don't you Mister Christian? You are one naughty Christian, don't you know."

He looked directly at her, smiled, rasped in a scratchy voice, "Yeah? Well you're the one dangling this little, um, apple at me, you know."

"Uh huh. I'm not giving it to you though. You can't have it."

"I can't? Not even a peek?"

"Nope."

"Okay," he said. "Not yet anyway."

How do you explain to an overweight ogre that such clever adolescent repartee with its attendant bursts of mindless giggles entitles you to lateness for supper, that mealtime tardiness or any other for that matter is fully justified by such harmless dabbling in nature's tender mysteries? Chris struggled up, patted off some of the dirt from the seat of his jeans. You can't, he thought.

Stretching, taking a deep breath, he mumbled, "Gotta go sometime."

"Shit," he added.

He walked down the half alley and entered the house he shared with his parents and a young sister, careful to guide the door to a silent close. As he climbed the three stairs to the main floor he heard a chair scrape the kitchen floor, his mother rising. Without hesitation he turned a corner and entered the kitchen, he appraised the scene as he approached his mother: she, large as a truck, standing there, hands on hips, glaring at him, lips tight, little Becky, his sister, already cowering over a plate of beans untouched, some chips, and a half eaten hot dog, an empty plate and a glass of milk, and a space where the old man would be sitting were he home. It didn't look good.

"Where the hell were you?"

"Out with friends. We didn't have a watch."

"Out with what friends?"

"Just friends."

"You," she said, turning to Becky. "Go to your room." The little girl slunk out of her chair and rushed past them and disappeared. Two paces separated Chris from his mother and she eliminated one of them. Before he could prepare for it he felt a blow alongside his head, his ear seemed to rupture like a blown truck tire, and a shrill ring blasted his consciousness. He lost his balance and fell sideways against the refrigerator, bright fractured lights darting across a black void behind his eyelids, he almost crumpled to the floor but caught himself, righted himself. He opened his eyes, tears were falling involuntarily, and what he saw through their distorting prism was a face crazy and otherworldly, an arm swinging. He ducked but it caught him at the scalp line and he lost his balance again.

She grabbed his shoulders and shook him. "You come in here late for supper and you tell me you're out with friends," she shouted. "I ask you what friends and you say just friends, you sassy little son of a bitch, you. Who do you think you are mouthing off to your mother like that, God damn you." She threw him away like a demented wrestler discarding a dummy. Off balance, he bounced off a wall and she caught him and he felt his hair in her hands and then felt the first contact of his head against the unyielding wall.

A chute opens and Chris slides like a torrent into an alternative universe, a universe at once familiar and startling and banal, a universe in which he finds all sensations suddenly and shatteringly indistinguishable, a universe uninhabited by any person but only force and effect, the force malicious unrelenting and incontestable that fuses roaring power and crushing sound into a furious unity with pain and thrust and imprecation, the whole emanating from a single source like darkness from nothing so that it (the effect) seems to the boy that it's the universe itself condemning him to hell in an incessant and reverberant propulsion that continues until he picks himself up from the floor and realizes that it was his mother doing all of that.

"Now get upstairs to your room and don't come down until I call you tomorrow morning, you sassy little shit," she bawled, and as he ran past her, mewling, with his arms covering his downturned head, one hand tight upon the other, she added, "I'll teach you to be a smart ass, you little son of a bitch."

The boy tore up the oak stairs, slipping once and banging his shin against a step but recovering quickly enough, he hurled himself the few paces to his room and caromed off the doorframe and dove onto the floor where he struggled to burrow legs first under his bed, his sanctuary for years, his refuge and his strength, his holy abode. When he started using it on such occasions as this, he was small enough to fall asleep and even change positions. Now that he had to squeeze in, his stay was temporary but nevertheless consoling. A sob escaped him and he felt the damp from his eyes and a stream of snot on his arms that his face rested on. From nipple to snot, he thought without mirth. From greenery to musty worn bedroom rug. All in such a short time, he mused. In just minutes, it seemed. He wondered, How does it all happen?

THE LONG, LIGHT EVENING

The shadows of leaves cast moving dapples against the richly textured bricks of the ell outside the kitchen window, and goldfinches and chickadees added dashes of vivacity and cheer as they flitted to and from the feeder dangling from a broad overhang. Talking on her portable phone before the sink and dishwasher, Esther Froman gazed at the birds, the lively shadows, the sweeping lawn that she kept so well watered and trimmed, the daisies and cosmos, the intense purple astilbes, standing tall and robust and delicate, aligned like sentinels before the nobility of the carefully pruned evergreens that formed the boundary of her property in the rear. Along the sunny side of the yard beyond the ell tomato plants grew almost noticeably against their six-foot high stakes, bejeweled with the green fruit that she loved so much, some in various stages of turning red; it was a good year so far, only the beginning of July and already her eight plants had yielded a dozen and a half juicy tomatoes which, sliced thickly and laid on toast in the mornings, salted slightly, served as her delicacy supreme, her taste of ecstasy that carried her through the hot summer days, the lonely nights.

Her yard was her first love. It was the lush greenness of the grass leaves, which she mowed with the carriage high and which consequently delighted the cottontails searching for the hidden clover, the little unafraid ones that Esther could barely see sometimes and the bigger ones, the timorous ones that darted away as soon as you stepped out the door, it was the squirrels leaving pathways, when the grass grew long, just before mowing time, the squirrels with their wit, their calculations, their avariciousness over spilt birdseed, it was the birds. It was the shadows of trees and the aliveness of summer breezes, it was the smell, always the smell, the smell of newness and energy in the grass, the lavender, the breeze sweeping in from the distant Great Lake, and it was the sounds, the glassy *shee-weet* of the finches, the rambling melodies of robins, the songs and sounds of all the life out there in her yard. It was these things that sustained Esther Froman, that made everything somehow worthwhile.

"Really, Rose. I want you to keep calling me when things come up. I'd like to join you tomorrow, but I just can't." Esther gazed at the grass, longed to sit in it now, her bare legs tickled by the long blades, the smooth softness. Just as soon as she got off the phone she'd go out there.

"But Esther," came the voice on the other end, "you say that all the time. I'm beginning to think you're breaking away."

"No, really." She felt a mild panic rising. "Really, Rose. I do want to be involved, but I just can't tomorrow. Things have been coming up lately. I can't help it. But I want to at least know what's going on. And believe me, I really do want to stay involved."

"That's okay, Esther. I believe you do."

There was a pause, Esther could hear a snap, a sharp intake of breath and an exhalation. Rose must have lit a cigarette, she thought. Still smoking. Well, don't say anything.

"Things going all right for you?" Rose asked. "You doing okay?"

"Of course. Things are going fine. I've just been really busy." Bickering sparrows occupied every perch on the feeder, others lined up on the roof, there was a regular chow line out there—finches and chickadees, a nuthatch or two, a downy woodpecker, chowing down before dark. Esther smiled with delight. "You should see the birds, Rosie. There's dozens of them out there, right outside my window."

Her head suddenly jerked and tilted back, her eyes rolled up and to the side. She abruptly cut off Rose's voice. "Excuse me, Rosie," she said. "I just heard something weird. I'll call you back in a little while."

She hung up and listened. A guttural noise, broken at short intervals like a sputtering motor at low idle, followed by a sharp raspy whine and then a mysterious whistle, fairly protracted but fading slowly, fading, fading, finally ending in stillness. It happened in the adjoining room, and Esther stood there looking toward it, at the half closed door, the leaves of a chiffolera plant against the fragment of wall visible through the crack, a plain round clock with hands at eight and five, twenty-five after eight, a section of a window frame. She clenched her teeth and pursed her thin lips, tweaked her nose, and took some cautious, measured steps toward the door. She swung it fully open. She saw Harvey across the room.

He was slumped in his leather chair, head tilted back, eyes

open, mouth slack. One elbow rested on a chair arm, the hand was raised, index finger raised a bit and arched. His legs were stretched out and resting on an ottoman, his ankles crossed. Impulsively, Esther looked upward, then returned her attention to her husband. His skin was whiter than his tee shirt, he sat as still as the rock on the table behind him. Esther seemed to play with her mouth, she pursed her lips again, drew them taut, rolled the bottom one down and then raised it over the top one. Her mouth thus sealed—she would not call out, certainly would not scream—her hands behind her back, she stepped forward, crossed the room, sat in the twin leather chair next to his. She gazed at him, her head nodding in a kind of rhythm, her eyes shifted to the overturned glass on his lap, the wet area of his pants, two ice cubes at his crotch and another on the seat. The clear bottle of scotch, newly opened, stood like a sentinel on the glass lamp stand beside his chair. Looking upon it, Esther formed her first thought.

"It finally gotcha, didn't it. It gotcha, and then it watched you die."

She watched impassively for signs that she was mistaken. She wanted to be certain. After a minute or two, she walked across the room, turned off the television without looking at the image on the tube, and returned with a castered desk chair, well cushioned with padded arms, she positioned it alongside his chair, the table lamp between them, and sat down. She slipped off her flip flops and set them aside neatly with her bare feet. And she looked at him. She wanted to be sure.

His mouth remained open but no sound came out, no vituperation, no scorn. It was quite lovely. His gray eyes were open, but there was no contempt in them, no ridicule; they were aimed upward and outward, but they saw nothing, she presumed, so there was nothing that she had to duck to avoid their bitter poisons. And there was his hand, raised as usual but not at her: at the air, with that bony index finger sticking out, but not jabbing her, no, but rather, wonderfully, bent, so that as she traced its trajectory it seemed to be directed at his own milky face. She smiled devilishly and nodded.

"Yeah," she thought, "don't you look like the fool this time."

The thought of calling 911 occurred to her, but she dismissed it. No, she had to be certain, absolutely positive. She'd wait for a while, maybe read some chapters of *Jane Eyre*, she was progressing nicely in it, reading it by day between gardening and lawn tending, between laundry washing and daydreaming. She liked to read in this room, in the chair Harvey's body was now occupying, this once formidable bulk reduced to a grotesque mannequin, but she couldn't read there in the evenings when he, besotted with predinner Manhattans and post-dinner scotches, and the television, vapid as his empty bottles, communed like impotent and hollow wastrels thrown together by a tasteless Fate. Or maybe she'd play a bit of solitaire on the nearby computer, an adequate time filler if ever there was one, one that often took her mind off her dread of his homecoming from work, his days flitting from one of his fast-food restaurants to another, overseeing the managers and greedily counting the rush hour customers, while she stayed home and, fully resigned to the banality of her role, waited for the weekly shopping allowance.

Must've been the heart attack we've been waiting for, she mused. Sure took long enough. He'd complained about his chest, some pains, sometimes fairly sharp, for weeks. And the shortness of breath. "Maybe I'd better have a doctor take a look at it or something," he'd say, sitting hunched on his bed in the early morning, panting heavily with his mouth open, grimacing occasionally as he grabbed his chest.

"I think you'd better," she'd reply. "But you'd better watch out, Harvey. He'll just give you a bunch of medications, blood thinners and the like, and tell you you can't drink anymore while you're taking them. And you'll have to take them the rest of your life."

Then the reaction, expected, unvarying, and, as Esther became more jaded, amusing: the spear-throwing eyes, brow tense as shrink wrap, the sharp inhalation, the tense, constricted neck. "You shut up, Esther, God damn it. What do you know about medicine anyway? You a goddamn doctor or something?" Sitting there, hunched and pathetic, half turned to show her his glower.

"No." Over the years it had become a game, and she had become good at it.

"You a goddamn RN or something?"

"No."

"No. God damn right, no. You're not even a goddamn LPN. You're not even a scrub tech or whatever they're called. A scrub. A goddamn orderly. So where you coming from, Esther, telling me that bullshit about medications? What do you know about medications anyway?"

"Nothing."

"God damn right, nothing. So keep your mouth shut about stuff you don't know nothing about. You understand what I'm saying? I don't need that from you, Esther, you hear me?""

At the rise in ferocity and volume, even in her memory, that always accompanied the last question, "You hear?" she started. Her eyes darted to his open mouth, his dull open eyes. It was as though the browbeating were being administered now, this minute, she sitting there still on guard and he occupying his throne before her, imperious and threatening; but when she saw his inert and waxen body she relaxed again, relieved. The dialogue was only in her brain again, repeated once more, she hoped for the last time now that he was no longer with her except in body. She smiled, raised her brow and tilted her head, looking sideways at the abhorrent corpse. He never did go for a checkup, she thought, as though revealing a secret to a friend, never got the cause of the chest pain diagnosed. For that matter he never got the occasional nagging pain just below the rib cage on his right side diagnosed either. The liver, she thought. She looked at the thing sitting there, closed her eyes and nodded rhythmically, opened them again, and she smirked.

She found *Jane Eyre* and decided to read for awhile. What a lovely book, she thought. She admired its language, at times mysterious and at others so wonderfully lilting, like the path of her finches from cedars to feeders, from feeders to bath, so different from the insipid TV diction, from her late husband's tiresome hectoring. But as she settled back to begin, she was struck by a sudden disturbing thought that made her hands slowly close the book.

She had killed Harvey. Of course she had. She had deliberately set him up for his heart attack. Yes, she thought. In what surely must have been moments of dread, even for one as reckless and insensitive as he, when he had actually thought of seeing a doctor she had each time over the course of weeks baldly suggested the one prescription for his certain refusal, out of the sheer obstinacy of his indomitable addiction, to get a checkup: that the doctor would insist he stop drinking. And each time he had completed his invective and stomped down the stairs and stormed out of the house, she knew, she knew: there would be no call for an appointment today. Or tomorrow. His indignation, his resentment, and his booze would take care of that.

Would he still be alive if she had encouraged him to seek a diagnosis for his worsening discomfort? Well. She gazed at the white stoney face. Probably, she concluded.

But he'd still be drinking too. On top of his meds. And then she'd have to nurse him through all the side effects. Yes. And she'd still have to take all his abuse, and listen to all his whining, yes. And she'd have to feel as though everything were all her fault, his abdominal pain and his badgering doctor and a healthy regimen impossible to follow, and he'd make her hate herself and make her feel so guilty, yes, so guilty, as he always does always does, and she couldn't take it any longer, she just couldn't, she'd go crazy, she'd, she'd...

"You...You, you..." she said aloud.

Her eyes fastened on his unmoving body, his upraised arm, she realized the rigidity of her own body, tense in his death as it had so often been in his life, and she breathed relief into herself, beginning with her eyes, blinking their way back into sanity, moving down to her shoulders and chest, and she sank back into the chair and stretched her legs. In a moment she was reading, determined to pass the time pleasurably until she was certain he was dead before calling 911. She read ten pages, read for about a half hour, and was doing pretty well, keeping her eyes trained on the flowing black letters, painting pictures in her imagination, enjoying Jane's happy preparations for her marriage to Mr. Rochester, her breathless anticipation, her state of rapture, when out of nowhere a twangy voice intruded in her reverie. The voice was country-sounding tenor, not her type of singing at all, but it and the lyrics from a song her son Tommy listened to years ago had etched themselves on her brain and now summoned a stream of tears and an involuntary snort that almost choked her.

> The devil will send demons
> To fly around your wedding day
> Yeah, the devil will send demons
> To fly around your wedding day…

The sudden intrusion of the words cut her deeply, she felt slashed open, disemboweled. They sure flew round me on my wedding day, she howled silently to herself. Her eyes closed tightly, her brows stretched upward, her nostrils dilated.

"But why?" she said aloud, then retreated again into the cavern of her own world, as though timid in front of the corpse before her. Why on my wedding day? What did I do? I never cheated on anybody else. I never hurt another boy, never disappointed another boy. I never even had another boy.

Suddenly, springing up and assailing her: an image long forgotten of haphazardly spaced teeth too large and uneven, a mouth too wide in a face too narrow, seen through almost lashless eyes damply returning her mirrored gaze on a dateless prom night, another barren night, a night without even a girlfriend to call, another in a lifetime of nights as a barren recluse. In a flash the image was gone but the empty feeling remained. And the word: Ugly.

Only Harvey, she thought. Only…

She sagged in resignation, fatigue. "You," she whispered. "You."

"You'll get your allowance on Thursday like you always do, you hear? On Thursday." Across twenty years his raspy voice, hurled at her as though she were a busboy at one of his restaurants asking for an advance, now abraded her like a skidding fall on pavement. Esther, too sad to wipe the tears seeping from her eyes, stared at him. *Jane Eyre* had slid off her lap and lay tentlike on the floor, its lovely narrative replaced with the memory of his harsh rattles, the reprise of a thousand old quarrels searing the evenings like lightning a hapless range lamb.

I should call Rose, she thought. I should call Rose. But her torpor clung to her, weighed her down. A thousand voices clamored in her darkness, fighting to be heard.

"But Harvey, the sale ends tomorrow and the dress is so pretty," her excited soprano said a quarter century ago. "You'll love me in it. It's black with lacey arms and a small slit, and the earrings and bracelet I saw to go with it…"

"God damn it, Esther, can't you understand what I'm saying to you? What's the matter with your head that you can't understand what the hell I'm saying to you?"

"But Harvey…"

"Are you so dense, Esther? Are you so goddamn dense that you can't understand what the hell I'm saying to you? No, Esther. Capital N capital O. That spells NO, Esther. And if you can't understand that, the NO means uh-uh, nope, naaah, it means bullshit, Esther, bullshit. Do you understand that, Esther?"

You never let me buy anything, you…you. She slashed away the remnants of her tears. Never. In forty-two years you never let me buy myself a dress by myself. You never let me do anything. The symphony. You never let me go to the symphony. I never had any money. "I give you an allowance, Esther. You've got plenty of money." Yeah, for food. For household stuff. For real pearls for your precious mother on her birthday. I get money to buy that. I get the money to buy gold cuff links for your daddy. You…you…

"I take care of you, Esther. Don't I take care of you? I take you on cruises, I buy you nice clothes, you got a nice house and a big yard. Look at that nice TV. Look at that nice sound system. I got you everything you need. What the hell you need a symphony for when you got that sound system?"

Hah, you got me everything I need, all right. Like a slaveholder. You got me what I needed to keep me around. The great beneficent master! Hah. You, you…You never let me get what I wanted. You never let me buy anything for myself. Unless you were there to approve, and to pay for it. My sugar daddy. Hah. The rest you spent on yourself buying up all those hookers with your buddies, and all those twenty and thirty dollar bottles of poison you poured down your sorry throat. I should have shown you. I should have gone out myself, sold myself. I could have sold myself as a goddamn dominatrix, could have pretended that every man I flayed and whipped was you. I could have made some decent money to spend on myself and maybe got some decent loving along the way, at least once in a while. You…

And how did Harvey always conclude his denial of her pleas for money? She heard his faraway voice in an echo: "And besides, you got me. Huh? Huh? You got me. Come on, right here, right now, right here on the table…"

Esther was tense now, her eyes on the body's hidden crotch. Only a trace of the spilt liquid remained on the garment that covered the thing the memory of which was making her lips curl. She was looking for a bulge, or at least the outline of something, but the baggy trousers laid only a slightly waved smoothness over the lap, offering some relief to her straining anger. Yeah, I had you, she thought. You only raped me for the last fifteen years of this god-forsaken marriage before you couldn't do it anymore, you, you, you…

"Bastard!"

Esther stopped, startled. Amazed. Did she say that? Aloud? Aloud? She had called him "bastard" many times, of course, and other words ever harsher. But never aloud. And certainly not to-night. Her tenseness melted, she smiled, she took a deep breath.

"Well," she said. "There."

In a moment she was in the kitchen and on the phone. "Rose? Rose, I'm sorry I took so long to call back. You know how it is, something comes up and you get lost in it and you just don't re-member to get back to the phone." Her friend Rose, her lovely friend, it was always such a comfort to talk with her, as pleasant as arranging her dahlias in vases, her zinnias, her lilies, her roses pink and red. It was dark outside now, and as they chattered away she absently watched her reflection in the window over the coun-ter where she stood, saw the room behind her illuminated in the glass, Harvey's crossed legs on the ottoman. The talk was light until Rose brought up the topic that they had shared for several years.

"Esther, are you okay? Are things going okay?"

"They're fine, Rose. Really.

"Harvey treating you okay?"

"Oh, it's been pretty much the same as usual. You know how it is."

"Esther. Um. You been going to your meetings lately?"

Esther smiled broadly. "Oh, not too much lately. Rose. I've been kind of neglecting them. Harvey gets so angry when I go to them, you know. Just livid. It's hard to live with that constant haranguing." She hesitated, smiled faintly. "But you know, I think I'll start up again. I think I'll start going a lot."

After a pause, Rose's voice sounded quiet with suppressed irritation. "I don't know how you can stand it, Esther. I would have left him years ago."

"I know it, Rose. I know it. But don't fret so much. I'm supposed to be the one fretting, not you. Besides, it'll all turn out okay. I know that." The closed smile gracing Esther's face opened like a flower, she could see her eyes glisten in the black window, her focus was on her image now, not Harvey's legs. "I promise, honey. I'll get back to my meetings and I'll get back to our committee work and I'll be just fine."

Back in the TV room, after rolling the chair back to the desk, she sat in front of the computer but had the chair facing the form of Harvey. She was slumped, relaxed, her legs extended and ankles crossed, hands resting on her thighs. She studied her feet, still youthful looking, uncalloused, toes still straight; all those years she had resisted Harvey's demands that she wear high heels, spikes, with the little pointy toed pump, she had succeeded in that, by God, she never once wore any, never even tried them on. Hah. That's all right, he probably got his fill of that fetish from all the whores and tramps he picked up over all those years. Her head shook at the thought, again her lips curled. Well, he never got me HIV-positive, anyway, she thought, whether he had it or not.

Her eyes roamed the length of her legs, free of varicose veins, still not heavy, though the knees were a bit rounded, like healthy mushroom caps, she thought. Some dimples. Slowly her fingertips began to roam the skin of her thighs, from the edge of her denim shorts down, along the sides, up the shorts to her crotch, roaming there, her fingers felt a bit of heat but there was nothing else, not a tingle, not a memory. She touched her breasts, her bra and the fabric of her plain shirt making them firmer than they were, but they were still nice, the nipples still surprisingly pink despite Harvey's mauling of them, despite their having nourished two children, Tommy and the other one, the dead one, poor little Paulie. She wondered whether they would someday register something, some sensation, some tickle, maybe a little thrill, something, until the blood really starts to flow again, the generators start to crackle. If they ever do again, she thought. If she ever gets past all this, this history.

Esther rotated the seat, faced the computer. She was going to play solitaire, but the sudden impulse to write something took control. To write something. To write. But what? She leaned forward, one elbow on the chair arm, her other arm akimbo, balled hand on her upper thigh. She stared, pursed her lips in the intense silence of the room, felt a sorrow surge from her belly to her throat, she raised her fingers to her lips, her eyes locked onto the keyboard. In a moment the program was running and her fingers were typing, two of them anyway, the index ones, typing in spurts between paralysis and revivification

Cows in the woods. October. Big yellow leaves in the maple forest. Big as dinner plates. Black and white cows, brown and white ones. In the woods. You were nervous, alone. I watched you from a dis-

tance. They were my woods. I knew every foot of them. Knew every rabbit hole, every stumper, where to find the slithery things. I watched you, proud and handsome. Searching for those little boys. Brothers. Searching all day. I caught up to you, watched you, your nervousness. I caught you finally. Remember your surprise? The lonely fire lane. Cows all around, milling around, some just standing there, chewing. Leaves blinding yellow. I put my hand in your big one and you said "You're here!" And then we stopped and we kissed and that was it, boy, that was it. We pulled off the fire lane—onto the big soft leaves, looked all around for cow plop, remember? Yellow leaves all over, smooth gray sky, oh I'll never forget it, all the cow onlookers."

She stopped, time stopped, she closed her eyes, remembering, picturing. Slowly she swiveled the chair around, covered her mouth with her slender fingers, opened her lids. Her mouth jerked open too and she gasped loudly. "Oh Harvey," she cried out. "You be my man again." She tightened her fingers over her mouth, then loosened them and let them slide down her chin. "You, you be my man again," she shouted. Then, in a hushed voice: "You just cross over that line and you be my man again."

His unresponsiveness drew a sigh from Esther and she sank back into her chair with a sigh and a snort of weariness. Hah, you never could take a demand from me, could you, she thought. It's been years since you showed the least bit of respect for me, you bastard, years! It wasn't so hard to call him bastard now; on the contrary, she seemed to relish the word, at least the ability to use it and get away with it. After a few more minutes of gazing at the cold body, she began to study details for the first time, disagreeable details, the things about his appearance that she despised but had come to suffer silently, preferring disgust to the humiliation she faced when bringing such matters to his attention. A carefully chosen set of words once uttered in a simpering tone such as, "Harvey, you know your nose hairs could use just a bit of trimming," would elicit a growling "What the hell's wrong with my nose hairs? They sticking out or something?" If she responded with a stuttering disclaimer, "W-w-well, no…no, not yet. But they're awfully close and they're awfully thick" (like dense gray pubes stuffed into a sink drain, she wanted to add), then he'd get the final word, still sophomoric even in his fifties and sixties: "Well, screw you, Miss Emily Goddamn Post. I like them. They keep my snot in and they keep all that spit that you spew in my face every time you open your mouth out."

"You've got to take care of yourself. You've got no control over him, his drinking, his insults. You can only take care of yourself," her friends at the twelve-step meetings she used to attend twice weekly always reminded her. "I know it, I know it," she bellowed inside. "But the words, the words, they just don't go away. They just don't go away. They keep coming back. How do you keep them from coming back?"

She wanted the whirling of Ravel, she got vitriol. She wanted the lyricism of Vivaldi, she got scurrility. "Turn that shit off, Esther, God damn it. What do you, you pretending to be highbrow or something? I don't need that shit. It aggravates me."

"But Harvey, can't I like anything? Can't I have any rights at all, not even to listen to the music I like?"

"Rights? Rights? Of course you got rights, Esther. Everybody in this country has rights, Esther. Don't you know that, Esther, for Chrissakes? This isn't a matter of rights, Esther. This is a matter of my coming home and needing some peace and quiet without listening to all that incessant freaking noise. I get noise all day at work and I don't need it when I walk into the sanctity of my freaking house. Is that all right with you, Esther, God damn it?"

Esther shut her eyes, hunched her shoulders, and shook her head quickly, as though shuddering from a sudden chill. She rose and crossed the room and peered at his features. "Look at it," she said aloud. "It's coming out your nose like whisk brooms. And the ears too. Looks like dried hay. You went to work like that today?" She put her hands on her hips like a disapproving mother. "And look at those eyebrows. Long and stiff as curtain rods." Lowering her head and drawing her lips tight, Esther turned and slowly trod to her chair, fatigue beginning to settle in. As she reached the chair she started as if touched from behind by a wraith.

"And who are you to judge me, Esther?" she heard his crackly voice shout from some distant past hallway. "Who the hell do you think you are, Miss Righteous, Miss Goddamn Holier-Than-Thou? I've put up with your judgmental looks for years and I'm sick of it. All you do is judge. You can't argue, you don't know the first thing about logic, you can't reason any better than a school kid, and you judge me?"

His mouth was cavernous, she could see the metallic fillings, his uvula swayed like a dangling tentacle, his breath—his breath, turbid with whiskey, foul, rank as sewage. But there it was, the image stark in her mind. As if the years had been erased she felt the force on her shoulder when she turned her head in disgust, the hard shove, she was falling before she realized it, she tried to scramble, catch herself, but she hit something, her ribs, the table corner, she saw the table hit her on the floor, then felt something else hard, on the head, stars blinked on a black field. She tried to get her bearings and sit up at the same time but floundered. Her forehead was wet, she felt and then saw blood dripping onto her skirt, onto the carpet, a heavy bodied lamp overturned beside her, the thing that hit her, the table on her leg, the jolts of pain and the confusion, Harvey's hysterical shouts, all that so long ago, so long ago. Seems like only yesterday.

And now a sudden wail tore through her throat and she cried without restraint, standing there leaning on the chair, her cascades of horror over the grief of her life pouring like floodwaters throughout the house. And when the flood had ebbed into sobs and she had soaked her hands in the salty fluid staining her cheeks, pooled in her eyes, she turned and stared at the body for a long time, heaving her breaths into gradual submission, gaining calmness, sighing into quiescence. She straightened her back, lifted her head, and breathed deeply.

"I'm okay," she said.

Seating herself, she pulled up solitaire on her computer and played a game and lost within twenty seconds. She had the program redeal and the game lasted longer. She played with an empty mind, and when his voice tried to intrude she stopped it. She could do that now, the flood finally having receded, the landscape empty, exhausted, waiting. She played game after game, making absolutely certain in her mind that he couldn't possibly be alive, and after she finally called 911 and called her son Tommy long distance to tell him the news and hear his dispassionate, laconic reply, she continued to play. She played until the doorbell rang, and she let the EMT people in courteously and to their comment about the apparent length of time that her husband seemed to have been dead, she said, "Yes, well, we occupy different ends of the house in the evening." At least one of them took notice of the game of cards on the monitor but said nothing, and in a little while they were gone and the space was hers alone.

The door closed and Esther stood there in silence, and the silence wrapped around her a panoply ethereal, recondite, but fully sensual, alive. Almost independently, her hand reached to the light switch and turned it off, and the darkness too surrounded her and it spoke to her in a voice clear and melodious as a cello, warm as a muffler, so that she, strangely, felt not at all alone in this silence, this dead of night. Listen, listen to this silence, it whispered, to the vastness of this circumambience, this endless universe. It's yours, Esther my dear, all yours.

Her eyes roamed the darkness, her lips parted, gradually black objects began to take shape against the black background. She heard creaks behind walls and breaths of wind outside, and she heard her own breath smooth and calm. She nodded gently.

"I've got to call Rose," she thought.

THE SOUL IN THERE

Hey, hey, it's stopped raining," the boy exulted, bursting through the doorway and out under the vine covered pergola on the flat roof of the great museum.

"Hey hey, and I see some patches of blue," his Uncle Richard shouted in his turn. It's going to clear up, my boy." The fleet rolling scud rushed past like a thick swarm of insects just above the tallest of the great buildings lining the horizon in the two visible directions, the blue patches as impermanent as a pinprick.

Chris stepped out into a shallow puddle left on the rectangular paving stones and turned his face into the breeze for a moment. "Feels good after all that time in there."

Uncle Richard joined him, face turned up and eyes closed as though he were under a shower head. "That it does. But you liked it in there, didn't you?" Hearing no answer, he turned and found the boy a dozen paces away at one of the featured artist's structures, an octagonal dome made of rough narrow rails, raw, unvarnished, and untreated, stacked horizontally, their ends resting on each other as on a log home but without notches, leaving several inches between each rail. Chris was peering through an eye-level crack at another structure within, a tower maybe twenty feet high made of smooth round stones one placed atop another, progressively smaller from a large base to what was no more than a large pebble which he could cup in his hand, like a knee, at the top. "It's like a soul in there," he thought. And then he wondered about this thought, skewing his face, as he surveyed the floor littered with ground stones, a loose sheet of paper. Everywhere, on the floor and on the tower, light and shadow played, shifted, modulated as the clouds raced along, thinning in their haste, letting in the sun, teasing it and then shutting it out again.

"You like that?" his uncle called to him. He hadn't left the pergola for watching the boy.

Chris turned to him, stepped away from the dome. "It's neat," he said.

"You know there's another one."

He approached his uncle, then turned and saw the second behind the first, identical in size and shape. He rushed over to it, noticing for the first time a few other museum visitors milling around. Stopping between the two domes, his head swiveled from one to the other, jerkily measuring their dimensions, shapes, content. "They're the same," he called.

His uncle nodded. "They're called *Stone Houses*."

Chris walked around the perimeter of each, then wandered onto the planked flooring of the roof as it extended to its southern border. Here he stopped, took a deep breath. His lips separated, his eyes grew as wide as when he first saw Karen's breasts last month, the last time, out of embarrassment and shame, she had permitted him to see any of her again. But what lay before him now was a substitute equally scintillating, miles of tree tops spread out to the south and west against a backdrop of buildings gray and tall and eerily stoic looking, stone solid against the whizzing clouds and the green vitality of the sea of trees.

"That's Central Park down there." It was his Uncle Richard's rich baritone. He felt a hand on his shoulder.

"It looks like, like…um. Broccoli," he asserted triumphantly. "Miles and miles of broccoli heads."

"You're right. It does," Uncle Richard seemed excited. "And beneath it all is traffic. Cars and buses and motorcycles. People walking and rollerblading. Dogs on leashes."

"Raccoons?"

Uncle Richard looked down at him. He smiled, nodded. "Yep. Of course. Lots of them."

In silence Chris raised his hand, and his hand took on a life of its own. It reached out and began to roam over the treetops and Chris's eyes and his head followed its smooth undulating flight like a bird's almost brushing the topmost leaves, gliding effortlessly on a current of freshly washed air, a refreshed cosmic sigh. He listened for the sounds down there, heard hums and coughs and sputters, but they probably came from the traffic on the adjoining Fifth Avenue, not from the creatures and vehicles burrowing under the trees of the park. Retrieving his hand, he gazed at it for a moment as if asking something of it, then let it roam again. The treetops seemed so delicate against the hard edges of the gray buildings beyond, but as he scanned the scene even they took on a new appearance, they seemed like guardians, a wall of guardians around the park, each building a skin around its denizens and all of them a skin around the park, with its broccoli tops a living parasol for the creatures thriving beneath. He looked to his side but his uncle was gone. Turning, he saw him on a bench near the pergola, head back, eyes closed, hands folded over his belly, just breathing. His eyes settled on the domes again, and in them through the tiny horizontal cracks he could make out fragments of the stone inhabitants, the earthy souls. He walked toward them slowly, measuring their growth against his casual approach. There was an evergreen hedge growing in a long planter that served as a rail, and he crouched low and from this perspective saw the dome rise from the greenery as if spawned by it. To the west rose also from the hedge two towers of a massive building far away on Central Park West. The hedge seemed to connect the towers to the dome in a long green passage, and Chris exhaled and held his breath.

"Uncle Richard," he called without movement. "Uncle Richard. Come here."

"Look, Uncle Richard. Crouch down and look," he said breathlessly when he saw a beige pantleg almost touching his side. "What does it look like?"

"My God," Uncle Richard said.

"It looks like some cathedral. I've seen pictures of a cathedral that this looks like."

"The Florence Cathedral."

"That's it. Yeah. Yeah. The Florence Cathedral. I saw pictures of it in my history book at school."

"Look at that. You're right. The dome is the same shape, even the ribs. Except the cathedral has only one tower."

"That's okay," Chris said. "Wow."

Uncle Richard returned to his bench. He'd seen all of this before, though not the cathedral illusion. He closed his eyes and was once more interrupted by Chris's voice, cracking in adolescent excitement. Again he rose and strode over to him, his eyes following the direction of the boy's outstretched arm. He saw a flagless vertical pole against a sky now mostly blue and still, and on the tip of that pole perched a large bird, majestic and motionless, from the top of this monument to civil sentiment, to universal vision and experience, surveying its domain of harnessed woodland, cultivated imitation of the wild with its outcroppings and paved trails and open grasslands and its broccoli trees. "Can you believe it?" shouted Chris.

"It's unbelievable?"

"How does this happen, Uncle Richard?"

"What's that, Chris?"

"Everything. All of this." His arm, independently alive, swiped over the whole scene. "And now the bird."

"It's a red-tailed hawk, Chris."

"The red-tailed hawk. And all the rest of this. How does it all happen to come together like this?"

Uncle Richard looked down at him. "Fate?" he said.

"You mean God?" asked Chris.

"I mean Fate. Whatever that is."

"Fate."

"It's either that or Chance, and I much prefer Fate."

He reached around the boy, gripped his shoulder. Chris felt the pressure and liked it. He stood transfixed, then his head began to move slowly, aimlessly, his eyes scanned the stolid buildings now quite glittering in the bright sunshine, the large domes before him, the stone towers inside them, the hawk, the sky, the broccoli trees.

He became acutely aware of the sound and feel of his breathing, felt something like a warm bubble swelling his face, his chest. "I can do that," he thought.

He stood stone still, all processes cerebral and corporeal in a state of unwitting suspension, only a fine emotion like a soft drizzle touching the edge of his consciousness, until he felt a pat on the shoulder and the abrupt withdrawal of his uncle. "I can do that," he repeated to himself. "All of it. I can." He raised his hands, gazed at them, gently interlocked the fingers and rested them against his stomach. I can take stuff and make any of this, all of it. Anything. Anything at all. He thought of dirt and bone and the smooth sheen of leaves, of gossamer wisps of hair and the ethereal softness of earlobes scented with the perfume of youth, he thought of shape and form and the exudation of life from wood and boulder, the malleability of flesh. All of this he thought and pictured, and then he walked to his uncle and sat beside him. "I can do all that," he said.

"All what, my boy?"

He held his arms out like a savior and he felt emotion fill his eyes. "All that."

Uncle Richard looked out there at all that and then at Chris. He tilted his head and sighed, twisted in his seat and extracted his wallet from his back pocket. He opened the wallet and took out a small piece of paper, unfolded it, said, "This is the only thought of mine I ever wrote down. It's the only thought I ever had that was worth writing down. I've always liked it." He offered it to Chris, who took it as if it held a mystery. There were two lines:

Life is fleeting, precious
Kiss the moment in art.

Chris read it, did a double take, his head snapped up to see his uncle who was gazing at the hawk, then it swirled leisurely like a curl of smoke along the plane of the sculptures to the buildings beyond, the green green treetops below, and up again to the hawk's perch and the white patches of clouds, high and starkly white against the forever azure.

I can do all that, he thought.